Praise for David G

Falling Out of Time

"Slim in dimension but as solid as sculpted rock. . . . Although it grows from a private, incomparable ordeal, this noble fable speaks for all."
—*The Independent* (London)

"Part narrative poem, part play, part novel . . . [a] poignant study of bereavement and loss."
—*Financial Times*

"Spare and poetic."   —*The New York Review of Books*

"The language of its composition makes it particular to Israel, but once translated [*Falling Out of Time*] becomes universal."
—*The Times Literary Supplement* (London)

"A haunting, affecting and even beautiful book. . . . [*Falling Out of Time*] resembles a play by Beckett or a Greek tragedy, in its empty setting, its direct existential subject matter, and even its form. . . . Although the book is weighted by sorrow, it's never cynical. Its tragedy is balanced by the beauty of the writing."
—*The Toronto Star*

"It's not a novel, but a mixture of poetry, prose and drama ... as true and as powerful as C. S. Lewis's great *A Grief Observed*."
                                    —*The Times* (London)

"A book that needed to be written. . . . Poetic. . . . [A] triumph."   —*The Observer* (London)

"A significant new departure in literature."
                                    —*Jewish Chronicle*

"At once more universal and more personal than anything [Grossman] has written before."
                                    —*Sunday Times* (London)

"*Falling Out of Time* is short, and clearly a deeply personal book, but its importance and impact ought not to be underestimated."   —*The Guardian* (London)

DAVID GROSSMAN

Falling Out of Time

David Grossman was born in Jerusalem, where
he still lives. He is the bestselling author of many
works of fiction, nonfiction, and children's literature, which have been translated into thirty-six
languages. His work has also appeared in *The New
Yorker*. He is the recipient of numerous awards,
including the French Chevalier de L'Ordre des Arts
et des Lettres, the Buxtehuder Bulle in Germany,
Rome's Premio per la Pace e l'Azione Umani-
taria, the Premio Ischia International Award for
Journalism, Israel's Emet Prize, and the Frankfurt
Peace Prize.

VINTAGE INTERNATIONAL

Falling Out of Time

Falling Out of Time

DAVID GROSSMAN

Translated from the Hebrew by Jessica Cohen

VINTAGE INTERNATIONAL
Vintage Books
A Division of Random House LLC
New York

FIRST VINTAGE INTERNATIONAL EDITION, DECEMBER 2014

Translation copyright © 2014 by Jessica Cohen

The Library of Congress has cataloged the Knopf edition as follows:
Grossman, David.
[Nofel mi-huts la-zeman. English]
Falling out of time / by David Grossman ; translated by Jessica Cohen.
— First edition.
pages cm
1. Bereavement—Fiction.   I. Cohen, Jessica.   II. Title.
PJ5054.G728N6413 2014
892.4'36—dc23   2013017532

Vintage Trade Paperback ISBN 978-0-345-80585-0
eBook ISBN 978-0-385-35014-3

Book design by Maggie Hinders

www.vintagebooks.com

Printed in the United States of America
10 9 8 7 6 5 4 3 2 1

Falling Out of Time

TOWN CHRONICLER: As they sit eating dinner, the man's face suddenly turns. He thrusts his plate away. Knives and forks clang. He stands up and seems not to know where he is. The woman recoils in her chair. His gaze hovers around her without taking hold, and she—wounded already by disaster—senses immediately: it's here again, touching me, its cold fingers on my lips. But what happened? she whispers with her eyes. Bewildered, the man looks at her and speaks:

—I have to go.
—Where?
—To him.
—Where?
—To him, there.
—To the place where it happened?
—No, no. There.
—What do you mean, there?

—I don't know.

—You're scaring me.

—Just to see him once more.

—But what could you see now? What is left
to see?

—I might be able to see him there. Maybe even
talk to him?

—Talk?!

TOWN CHRONICLER: Now they both unfold,
awaken. The man speaks again.

—Your voice.

—It's back. Yours too.

—How I missed your voice.

—I thought we ... that we'd never ...

—I missed your voice more than I missed
my own.

—But what is *there*? There's no such place. *There*
doesn't exist!

—If you go there, it does.

—But you don't come back. No one ever has.

—Because only the dead have gone.

—And you—how will you go?

—I will go there alive.

—But you won't come back.

—Maybe he's waiting for us.
—He's not. It's been five years and he's still not.
  He's not.
—Maybe he's wondering why we gave up on him
  so quickly, the minute they notified us . . .
—Look at me. Look into my eyes. What are you
  doing to us? It's me, can't you see? This is us,
  the two of us. This is our home. Our kitchen.
  Come, sit down. I'll give you some soup.

MAN:
Lovely—
So lovely—
The kitchen
is lovely
right now,
with you ladling soup.
Here it's warm and soft,
and steam
covers the cold
windowpane—

TOWN CHRONICLER: Perhaps because of the
long years of silence, his hoarse voice fades to a
whisper. He does not take his eyes off her. He
watches so intently that her hand trembles.

MAN:
And loveliest of all are your tender,
curved arms.
Life is here,
dear one.
I had forgotten:
life is in the place where you
ladle soup
under the glowing light.
You did well to remind me:
we are here
and he is there,
and a timeless border
stands between us.
I had forgotten:
we are here
and he—
but it's impossible!
Impossible.

WOMAN:
Look at me. No,
not with that empty gaze.
Stop.
Come back to me,
to us. It's so easy
to forsake us, and this

light, and tender
arms, and the thought
that we have come back
to life,
and that time
nonetheless
places thin compresses—

MAN:
No, this is impossible.
It's no longer possible
that we,
that the sun,
that the watches, the shops,
that the moon,
the couples,
that tree-lined boulevards
turn green, that blood
in our veins,
that spring and autumn,
that people
innocently,
that things just are.
That the children
of others,
that their brightness
and warmness—

WOMAN:
Be careful,
you are saying
things.
The threads
are so fine.

MAN:
At night people came
bearing news.
They walked a long way,
quietly grave,
and perhaps, as they did so,
they stole a taste, a lick.
With a child's wonder
they learned they could hold
death in their mouths
like candy made of poison
to which they are miraculously
immune.
We opened the door,
this one. We stood here,
you and I,
shoulder to shoulder,
they
on the threshold
and we

facing them,
and they,
mercifully,
quietly,
stood there and
gave us
the breath
of death.

WOMAN:
It was awfully quiet.
Cold flames lapped around us.
I said: I knew, tonight
you would come. I thought:
Come, noiseful void.

MAN:
From far away,
I heard you:
Don't be afraid, you said,
I did not shout
when he was born, and
I won't shout now either.

WOMAN:
Our prior life
kept growing

inside us
for a few moments longer.
Speech,
movements,
expressions.

MAN AND WOMAN:
Now,
for a moment,
we sink.
Both not saying
the same words.
Not bewailing him,
for now,
but bewailing the music
of our previous life, the
wondrously simple, the
ease, the
face
free of wrinkles.

WOMAN:
But we promised each other,
we swore to be,
to ache,
to miss
him,

to live.
So what is it now
that makes you
suddenly tear away?

MAN:
After that night
a stranger came and grasped
my shoulders and said: Save
what is left.
Fight, try to heal.
Look into her eyes, cling
to her eyes, always
her eyes—
do not let go.

WOMAN:
Don't go back there,
to those days. Do not
turn back your gaze.

MAN:
In that darkness I saw
one eye
weeping
and one eye
crazed.

A human eye,
extinguished,
and the eye
of a beast.
A beast half
devoured in the predator's mouth,
soaked with blood,
insane,
peered out at me from your eye.

WOMAN:
The earth
gaped open,
gulped us
and disgorged.
Don't go back
there, do not go,
not even one step
out of the light.

MAN:
I could not, I dared not
look into your eye,
that eye of
madness,
into your noneness.

WOMAN:
I did not see you,
I did not see
a thing,
from the human eye
or the eye
of the beast.
My soul was uprooted.
It was very cold then
and it is cold
now, too.
Come to sleep,
it's late.

MAN:
For five years
we unspoke
that night.
You fell mute,
then I.
For you the quiet
was good,
and I felt it clutch
at my throat. One after
the other, the words
died, and we were
like a house

where the lights
go slowly out,
until a somber silence
fell—

WOMAN:
And in it
I rediscovered you,
and him. A dark mantle
cloaked the three of us,
enfolded us
with him, and we were mute
like him. Three embryos
conceived
by the bane—

MAN:
And together
we were born
on the other side,
without words,
without colors,
and we learned
to live
the inverse
of life.

(silence)

WOMAN:
See how
word by word
our confiding
is <u>attenuated</u>, macerated,
like a dream
illuminated
by a torch. There was
a certain miracle
within the quietude,
a secrecy
within the silence
that swallowed us up
with him. We were silent there
like him, there we spoke
his tongue.
For words—
how does the drumming
of words voice
his death?!

TOWN CHRONICLER: In the hush that follows her
shout, the man retreats until his back touches
the wall. Slowly, as if in his sleep, he spreads both

arms out and steps along the wall. He circles the small kitchen, around and around her.

MAN:
Tell me,
tell me
about us
that night.

WOMAN:
I sense something
secret: you are tearing off
the bandages
so you may drink
your blood, provisions
for your journey to *there*.

MAN:
That night,
tell me
about us
that night.

WOMAN:
You
circle
around me

like a beast
of prey. You close
in on me
like a nightmare.
That night, that
night.
You want to hear about
that night.
We sat on these chairs,
you there, me here.
You smoked. I remember
your face came
and went in the smoke,
less and less
each time. Less
you, less
man.

MAN:
We waited
in silence
for morning.
No
morning
came.
No
blood

flowed.
I stood up, I wrapped you
in a blanket,
you gripped my hand, looked
straight into my eyes: the man
and woman
we had been
nodded farewell.

WOMAN:
No
wafted dark
and cold
from the walls,
bound my body,
closed and barred
my womb. I thought:
They are sealing
the home that once
was me.

MAN:
Speak. Tell me
more. What did we say?
Who spoke first? It was very quiet,
wasn't it? I remember breaths.
And your hands twisting

together. Everything else
is erased.

WOMAN:
Cold, quiet fire burned
around us.
The world outside shriveled,
sighed, dwindled
into a single dot,
scant,
black,
malignant.
I thought: We must
leave.
I knew: There's nowhere
left.

MAN:
The minute
it happened,
the minute
it became—

WOMAN:
In an instant we were cast out
to a land of exile.
They came at night, knocked on our door,

and said: At such and such time,
in this or that place, your son
thus and thus.
They quickly wove
a dense web, hour
and minute and location,
but the web had a hole in it, you
see? The dense web
must have had a hole,
and our son
fell
through.

TOWN CHRONICLER: As she speaks these words,
he stops circling her. She looks at him with dulled
eyes. Lost, arms limp, he faces her, as if struck at
that moment by an arrow shot long ago.

WOMAN:
Will I ever again
see you
as you are,
rather than as
he is not?

MAN:
I can remember
you without
his noneness—your innocent,
hopeful smile—and I can remember
myself without his noneness. But not
him. Strange: him
without his noneness, I can no longer
remember. And as time goes by
it starts to seem as though
even when he was,
there were signs
of his noneness.

WOMAN:
Sometimes, you know,
I miss
that ravaged,
bloody
she.
Sometimes I believe her
more than I believe
myself.

MAN:
She is the reason I take
my life

in your hands and ask
you a question
I myself
do not understand:
Will you go with me?
There—
to him?

WOMAN:
That night I thought:
Now we will separate. We cannot live
together any longer. When I tell you
yes,
you will embrace
the no, embrace
the empty space
of him.

MAN:
How will we cleave together?
I wondered that night.
How will we crave each other?
When I kiss you,
my tongue will be slashed
by the shards of his name
in your mouth—

WOMAN:
How will you look into my eyes
with him there,
an embryo
in the black
of my pupils?
Every look, every touch,
will pierce. How will we love,
I thought that night.
How will we love, when
in deep love
he was
conceived.

MAN:
The
moment
it happened—

WOMAN:
It happened? Look
at me, tell me:
Did it happen?

MAN:
And it billows up
abundantly,

an endless
wellspring. And I
know—as long as
I breathe,
I will draw
and drink and drip
that blackened
moment.

WOMAN:
Mourning condemns
the living
to the grimmest solitude,
much like the loneliness
in which disease
enclothes
the ailing.

MAN:
But in that loneliness,
where—like soul
departing body—
I am torn
from myself, there
I am no longer alone,
no longer alone,
ever since.

And I am not
just one there,
and never will be
only one—

WOMAN:
There I touch his
inner self,
his gulf,
as I have
never touched
a person
in the world—

MAN:
And he,
he also touches
me from
there, and his touch—
no one has ever
touched me in that way.

(silence)

WOMAN:
If there were such a thing
as *there,*

and there isn't,
you know—but if
there were,
they would have already gone
there.
One of everyone would have
got up and gone. And how
far will you go,
and how will you know
your way back,
and what if you don't
come back, and even if
you find it—
and you won't,
because it isn't—
if you find it, you will not
come back,
they will not let you
back, and if you do
come back, how
will you be, you might
come back so different
that you won't
come back,
and what about me,
how will I be if you don't
come back, or if

you come back
so different that you don't
come back?

TOWN CHRONICLER: She gets up and embraces
him. Her hands scamper over his body. Her
mouth probes his face, his eyes, his lips. From
my post in the shadows, outside their window, it
looks as if she is throwing herself over him like a
blanket on a fire.

WOMAN:
That night I thought:
Now we will never
separate.
Even if we want to,
how can we?
Who will sustain him, who will
embrace
if our two bodies do not
envelop
his empty fullness?

MAN:
Come,
what could be simpler?
Without mulling or wondering

or thinking: his mother
and father
get up and go
to him.

WOMAN:
In whose eyes will we look to see him,
present and absent?
In whose hand
will we intertwine fingers
to weave him
fleetingly
in our flesh?
Don't go.

MAN:
The eyes,
one single
spark
from his eyes—
how can we,
how may we
not try?

WOMAN:
And what will you tell him,
you miserable madman?

What will you say? That hours
after him, the hunger awoke
in you?
That your body
and mine, like a pair
of ticks, clutched
at life and clung
to each other and forced us
to live?

MAN:
If we can be with him
for one more moment,
perhaps he, too,
will be
for one more
moment,
a look—
a breath—

WOMAN:
And then what?
What will become
of him?
And of us?

MAN:
Perhaps we'll die like he did, instantly.
Or, facing him, suspended,
we will swing
between the living
and the dead—
but that we know. Five years
on the gallows of grief.

(pause)

The smell
from your body
when your anguish
plunges on you,
lunges;
the bitter smell in which
I always find
his odor, too.

WOMAN:
His smells—
sweet, sharp,
sour.
His washed hair
his bathed flesh

the simple spices
of the body—

MAN:
The way he used to sweat after a game,
remember?
Burning with excitement—

WOMAN:
Oh, he had smells for every season:
the earthy aromas of autumn hikes,
rain evaporating from wool sweaters,
and when you worked the spring fields together,
odor from the sweat of your brows,
the vapors of working men, filled the house—

MAN:
But most of all I loved the summer,
with its notes of peaches
and plums,
their juices running down his cheeks—

WOMAN:
And when he came back
from a campfire with friends,
night and smoke
on his breath—

MAN:
Or when he returned
from the beach,
a salty tang
in his hair—

WOMAN:
On his skin.
The scent of his baby blanket,
the smell of his diapers
when he drank only breast milk,
then seemingly
one moment later—

MAN:
The sheets of a boy
in love.

WOMAN:
Sometimes, when we are
together, your sorrow
grips my sorrow,
my pain bleeds into yours,
and suddenly the echo of
his mended, whole body
comes from inside us,

and then one might briefly imagine—
he is here.

(pause)

I would go
to the end
of the world with you,
you know. But you are not
going to him, you are going
somewhere else, and there
I will not go, I cannot.
I will not.
It is easier to go
than to stay.
I have bitten my flesh
for five years
so as not to go, not
there,
there is
no *there*!

MAN:
There will be,
if we go
there.

TOWN CHRONICLER: She looks away from him.
They are distant, as though he is no longer here,
on this side. He takes a deep breath, inhaling the
small kitchen and the entire house, and her—her
face, her body. Then he straightens up. As he
walks past, his hand rests briefly on her waist,
barely touching. He leaves the house and shuts the
door behind him.

And stops: the sky is low and black, the broad-
chested night pushes him back to the house.
He looks at the closed door. His feet hesitate,
probing. He walks—strange—orbiting himself in
a small circle. Slowly, carefully, again and again,
one circle after another. His arms spread out,
the circles grow wider, he walks around the small
yard, and now he circles the house—

WALKING MAN:
Here I will fall
now I will fall—

I do not fall.

Now, here,
the heart
will stop—

It does not stop.

Here is shadow
and fog—
now,
now
I will fall—

TOWN CHRONICLER: The night air is damp and
cool. Clouds roll over the big swamps in the east,
covering the stub of moon. Again and again he
circles the house, as if hoping his motion will
rouse her and enthuse her.

WALKING MAN:
Your icy voice
ensnarls
my feet. How will I walk
without your warmth, without the light
of your eyes?
How will I walk
if you withhold
your grace?

TOWN CHRONICLER: His gaze always fixed on
the shuttered blinds, he circles the house again

and again, but gradually moves farther away. He
opens up, spreads out, walking farther, farther,
his circles growing larger and wider. He walks
there—there is no *there*, of course there isn't,
but what if you go there? What if a man walks
there?

WALKING MAN:
I am not alone, I am not
alone, I whisper
like an oath,
and his breath
through my mouth
clouds the mirror.
I am not alone,
with him I am
not alone—

TOWN CHRONICLER: He gradually encircles the
whole village, then he does so again. He walks
by houses, yards, wells, and fields, past barns and
paddocks and woodpiles. Dogs bark at him and
quickly retreat with a whimper, and he walks.

WALKING MAN:
I am not alone. With him
I am not *one*,

I am alone
with him in all
my thickets, my labyrinths.
He pulses in me, lives
with me, one
with me, with him
I share the vast expanse his death
created in me—
and he surges
and he wanes with me,
unquiet
unquiet
roaming
embittering
redeeming
shackling
healing
purifying,
not letting go,
not letting go,
this
lonely
dead
child.

TOWN CHRONICLER: Night after night after night.
Things are happening in your town, my lord, and

I fear I will not have the time to record them all for you.

Right now, at midnight, at the old wharf by the lake, something stirs inside a skein of fishing nets. A head pokes out and glances around. A tiny, supple body pulls itself out of the skein and sits up breathlessly. It is a person, undoubtedly. Frightened eyes gleam white in the filthy face as they scan the hilltops surrounding the town. The gaping mouth turns to look, like a dark third eye.

Now I see: it is the net-mender. You may recall, Your Highness, that years ago, on one of your visits to the harbor, you enjoyed her sharp tongue when she argued with you over the needle tax you had levied, in your benevolence, at the time. A cheerful, curly-haired boy was tied to her chest in a brightly colored sling. He played a game of peekaboo with you, and you gave him a gold coin. I do not know what became of him. From time to time I see her roaming the streets near the harbor, grunting, muttering unintelligible words to herself, encumbered by a tangled web of fishing nets that makes one wonder whether there is a human being inside at all.

She suddenly leaps up as if snakebitten. Her hands rise and she points far away. She groans—

If you are awake, my lord, and would be so kind

as to look out of your window, you, too, will see:
a small luminance of sorts encircles the town. A
man walks there, up and down the hills.

WALKING MAN:
One step,
another step, another
step,
walking and
walking to you.
I am
an unleashed question,
an open shout

My son

If only
I could
move
you
just
one
step.

TOWN CHRONICLER: And on the third night
watch, in a side alley on the outskirts of town, in
a little house with one room, a centaur sits at a

table. That is what the townsfolk call him, Your
Highness, and I promise to try to find out why
very shortly. His massive head, adorned with
snowy-white curls, droops onto his chest. His
spectacles have slid down to the edge of his nose,
and his snores shake the house. I glance right
and left: no one. I rise up on my toes and peer
inside. The room is dusky, but I can discern that
it is overflowing: strange mounds and heaps that
might be dirt or garbage, or piles of old furniture,
surround the man and at times reach the ceiling.
It is hard to see how he can move in this room.

A dirty blanket is spread out on the desk before
him. A few empty beer bottles, pens, pencils,
a school notebook, all scattered around. The
notebook is open; its pages have thin blue lines.
As best I can tell from here, they are all empty.

"Scram before I wring your balls," the centaur
growls without opening his eyes, and I flee for my
life.

Only when I reach the fence outside the home
of the woman from whom I have exiled myself
does my heart recover.

TOWN CHRONICLER'S WIFE:
The passing time
is painful. I have lost

the art
of moving simply,
naturally, within it.
I am swept back
against its flow. Angry, vindictive,
it pierces me
all the time, all the
time
with its
spikes.

TOWN CHRONICLER: The next evening, in a
hut in a slum on the outskirts of town, a young
woman—trained as a midwife—gets up abruptly
from her kneeling position by a tub of water and
stands with her hands dripping. As far as I can
see, there is no laboring woman in the room, nor a
baby. Only a man's trousers and shirt float in the
tub. The woman freezes. Her neck is a stalk, her
face long and gentle. Somewhat rigidly, she turns
and walks to the window. Outside it is cold and
stormy, and since the chimney emits no smoke—
allowing me to peer through it—I assume it is
very cold inside, too.

Her gaze probes the faraway hilltops on
the horizon. She is silent, but her fingers rend
her mouth apart as if in a scream, until I hold

my breath as well. When she finally sighs, her shoulders collapse, as though her strength has suddenly left her.

Her husband—barrel-chested, with a reddish shaved skull and three thick folds on the back of his neck—who all this time has sat in the corner cobbling a pair of riding boots, punctuating and vowelizing her silence with the rapid blows of his hammer, hisses through the nails in his mouth:

COBBLER: Poisoning your soul again?

MIDWIFE: Y-y-yesterday she w-w-would have been f-f-five.

COBBLER: I've told you a hundred times not to think about these things! Enough, it's over!

MIDWIFE: I lit a candle by her p-p-picture and you said n-n-nothing. Don't you ever think about her?

COBBLER: What is there to think? How much of a life did she even have? A year?

MIDWIFE: And a h-h-half.

TOWN CHRONICLER: The cobbler slams the boot heel with his hammer as hard as he can, curses, and with peculiar lust sucks the blood that spurts from his finger.

Heavy with thought, I leave. The town is asleep; its streets are empty. At the edge of the old wharf I stop and wait. The leaden clouds almost touch the water. Daybreak will soon come.

As she did last night, the mute net-mender thrusts her head out of the skein. She looks around, searching, as if a voice had called her. I hide behind a lamppost. She suddenly leaps and runs down the pier with unbelievable speed, past skeletons of boats and rusty anchors, her long nets dragging behind her, floating.

On the wooden bridge she stops. I can hear her breath whistling. Who knows what is plaguing this miserable creature's mind? She grabs the railing and rocks it wildly. How much force and fury that little frame contains! I carefully move closer and crouch behind an overturned boat. The lake is turbulent tonight, and it sprays my glasses with droplets. In such moments, Your Highness, I practically curse my blind obedience to your orders. It is hard to see from here, but it seems as though someone is trying to force the mute to turn back and look at the hills, and she fights him

and grunts and spits, squirming as her tiny, supple
body is tossed from side to side. I write quickly
in the dark my hand is trembling I apologize
for the handwriting Your Highness perhaps she
is about to throw herself into the lake and then
what will I do it's been so many years since I've
touched anyone and her head at once pulls sharply
back maybe there really is someone in the dark
breaking her neck—

Her mouth gapes, teeth exposed, and suddenly
all is quiet. How such silence and the lake as if the
waves do not

MUTE WOMAN IN NET:
Two human specks,
a mother and her child,
we glided through the world
for six whole years.

TOWN CHRONICLER: Astonished, she plunges once
again into the mess of nets. I am exceedingly cold,
Your Highness. Such phenomena disquiet me.
The lake coming back to life so suddenly, and the
boats once again knocking into one another and
creaking in mockery. You will ridicule me, too, my
lord, but I am willing to swear that I saw a slim
band of light coming out of her mouth. Perhaps

just a moonlight apparition. But there is no moon
tonight. And the fact that for one moment, when
she sang, she was almost beautiful . . . I am merely
reporting. Her voice was clear. I might even
venture to say: heavenly. But what do I know?
I am tired. This is all so confusing. Perhaps I
should take a nap in one of the boats

    Wait—

    Like a quick little animal she burrows into her
nets and is gone. According to the records in my
possession she has not uttered a single word for
upward of nine years.

    And now, Your Highness, it is finally dawn.

DUKE:
Dawn!
From within the loathsome
night,
from the theater
of its nightmares, I once again
extract and
collect myself piece
by piece, a monarch-
mosaic: here is my hand
outstretched for bread,
and its fresh smell
and warm body,

but first, first
my eye
goes to the window,
drawn to two birds in a puddle,
to a dawn rising
sanguine. Look, *optimistic or poor in a bad*
my lord, you are blessed: *situation*
here on a platter
is a newborn day,
its teeth not yet emerged—

But for a week now, far away
on the hilltops, a man
like an open razor blade walks
and cuts, his head
in the sky.

WALKING MAN:
And yet
I shall move you,
my rootless child,
my cold,
fruitless child.
Every day it gets
harder, every day you grow
more hardened, more
and more taxing.

TOWN CHRONICLER: Every time the midwife leaves the room, the cobbler jumps up to the window. His eyes dart over the hills, his lips seem to chew up insults and curses. Hammer in hand.

He notices me in his yard now, behind an empty chicken coop. He does not come out or banish me; he doesn't even threaten me with his hammer. I carefully show him my notebook and pen. I believe I see him nod.

MIDWIFE:
Opposite my bed
on the w-w-wall
is an ancient round
c-c-clock.
It is old and weak,
with hands s-s-stuck
on the same hour
and the same m-m-minute
for more than a y-y-year—

TOWN CHRONICLER: Her voice, soft and flat, comes from the next room. The cobbler moves away from the window. He walks backward. Backward? Strange: as if sleepwalking, he probes around until his back touches the wall. Both arms slowly rise on either side. His shaved red head

slams against the wall to the beat of the words
from the other room.

MIDWIFE:
And only
the thin s-s-second
hand keeps fluttering
p-p-pouncing all the time
all the time that's
left, all the time
that was given,
p-p-pounces and lurches
back
unw-w-wavering,
storming
fighting
to pass
to cross
or just
t-t-to be,
to be one sheer full simple second no more no less
just that, God,
just be.

DUKE:
And here, in the palace,
in the private chamber,

a whistling kettle and steaming
coffee. I am serene and slow
and limp, undoubtedly:
an exemplary duke—
no.
No.
A man not-himself
has awoken from this night—
all hollow bones,
hah, the gravity
of tragedy. (You thought
you were safe, m'lord, you thought you were
immune. Your troops
cover the land, a thousand hussars
on a thousand horses, and you in
shattered shards.) But he rises,
he rises to his day,
silently puts on the slough
of his name, inwardly
fans the dim embers, does his best
to convince himself that he still remembers
what it was like to
just
be;
how to stare, for example,
how to stare? How
does a person just stare

innocently, how does he
for one instant forget
what is seared inside him
by affliction?
In short—
an impostor of sorts, a sham,
pretending to be an everyman
whose eye
is drawn to the open window, whose hand
reaches simply
for bread—

Amid all this, I suddenly
plummet,
plunge,
a mere
shadow
of he who walks there
alone, of he who,
with heavy steps,
chisels the verdict
on my land:
all that is,
all that is
(oh, my child,
my sweet, my lost one)—

all that is
will now
echo
what is not.

TOWN CHRONICLER: "It's like a murmur," the
centaur explains when I pass by his window the
next evening. "A murmur, or a sort of dry rustle
inside your head, and it never stops."

Not willingly, Your Highness, does he give his
testimony. Only after I show him the royal edict
with your seal and portrait does he realize that he
has no choice but to collaborate.

CENTAUR: "*Veritably*"? You need to know what's
going on with me? You're telling me the duke
could give two shits about what is *veritably*
buzzing around in my head? Okay, then, gird
your gonads and do some chronicling. Write
down that it's, let's say, like dry leaves. What are
you ogling at like an idiot? Leaves! But dry ones,
right? Crumbling. Dead. Did you get that? And
someone keeps stepping on them, over and over
again . . . So? Is that *veritable* enough for you? Will
the duke be pleased? Will his face glisten with
delight?

TOWN CHRONICLER: My own honor, my lord, is easily put aside. But I am absolutely unwilling to allow *your* representative to be humiliated this way, and so I immediately turn to leave—

CENTAUR: What's that? Without a kiss? Get back here right now! I believe, pencil pusher, that your edict explicitly requests *"all the information required for the authorities, without omitting a single detail"*! True or false? Well then, open up your little notebook right this minute and start chronicling:

"Someone keeps treading on them, on the dry leaves"—write this!—"walking around and around in a circle, dragging his feet . . ." Now make a note of this: *khrrrsss khrrrsss.* Like that, yes, with three *s*'s at the end. I bet that little detail will clarify the situation for the duke *veritably*! That will get it up for him in no time! Are you getting the picture, lap-clerk? Has anyone ever told you your face looks like a waif's?

TOWN CHRONICLER: While I pretend to be writing down this foolish drivel, I periodically stand on my tiptoes to steal a glance at the heaps crammed into his room. I make a quick list: wooden cradle, pram, tiny bed, lots of deflated

soccer balls, colorful little chairs, rocking horse,
toy boat, rusty cars from an electric train,
cowboy hat, Indian feather chain, endless pages
of drawings and doodles . . . Incidentally, this
whole assemblage is covered with fly droppings
and cobwebs. It all seems withered and brittle,
and every object looks as though it might crumble
at the slightest touch, if not a mere look. The
creature in the window keeps on prattling,
cursing, and slandering. I persist. Gym shoes,
skates and sandals, books, books everywhere, a
small school desk, pencil cases, a green chamber
pot, a little bicycle with training wheels . . .
He can blather on all he wants with his filthy
curses. I nod at him once in a while. Even twenty
notebooks would not suffice. This place contains
an entire museum of childhood—or perhaps
the museum of one child. Rubber fins and swim
goggles, wool teddy bears, furry lions and tigers—

He's stopped talking. He peers over his glasses
at me. He might suspect something. A little
accordion, backpack, tin soldiers, paintbrushes,
not good, I am disquieted, those bloodshot
eyes. I'll stop soon. Hey, board games! Beloved
Monopoly, Snakes and Ladders, decks of cards,
props for the budding magician, Boy Scout

uniform, goody bags from birthday parties, bow and arrow—how can you even breathe in this room?

CENTAUR: You can't. And now, if you value your life, hireling, get lost and don't come back. Off you go! Pronto!

TOWN CHRONICLER: Picture albums, masks, toy gun, pacifiers, whistles, flashlight—

CENTAUR: Scram, you leech! Otherwise I'll come out to you—

WOMAN WHO STAYED AT HOME:
Five years after my son
died, his father went out
to meet him.
I did not go with him.
I did not go. I did not go so much
that I foundered. I sat
cross-legged, displaced. I listened
to a voice that reached me
from afar: he
walks, he walks. I did
not go.
I did not.

Not
there.
My heart beat:
he walks. My blood
pounded: he walks.
Spoons and forks clattered, mirrors
glittered, signaled: see
him, see him, day and night, he
walks. I would go with him
to the end
of the world. Not there,
not
there.

DUKE:

 . . . he might be an insurgent; I am
uncertain. My scouts say
he poses a danger:
the coolness of the unruly, of a
stubborn, wayward man.
But his eyes—they report—
shine with the pale blue light
of a child's gaze.

MIDWIFE:
You will n-n-never know,
my d-d-daughter, that every man

is an island,
that you c-c-cannot know another
from within. A son's own
mother cannot
be him, even for an instant,
cannot sustain
him, self-sustain herself
in him—

TOWN CHRONICLER: The town streets are thick
with fog. The midwife is at her window, her eyes
on the hills, her lips almost kissing the pane as
she whispers feverishly. Fragmented vapors
appear on the glass like hieroglyphics and quickly
vanish, sometimes before I can write them down.
From my post—this time behind the crumbling
well in the yard—I notice her husband sitting
on his stool, watching her longingly, hammer in
hand.

MIDWIFE:
Nor will m-m-my self adhere
to your self any longer,
nor will my self
to myself adhere. It has all come apart. They say
there are things in the world. They say things
are c-c-connected. I look in the f-f-faces

of those who say, and see
holes
and crumbs,
specks
of limbs.

CENTAUR: He keeps stepping on the leaves in
my mind, trampling them, day and night, always
the same rhythm, never changing, fifteen years
it's been, since *then,* even when I sleep, when I
shit, yes, write that down, it should be written
somewhere, and there are whispers, too, all the
time, like this: *Hmmm . . . hmmm . . .* And then he
lunges like a swarm of wasps, *buzzzzzzzz,* drilling
through my brain: it happened, it happened, it
happened to him, it's forever, it's forever, and he
won't, he'll never—

    Ummm, look, lackey, this is just inside me,
right? You can't hear it, can you?

TOWN CHRONICLER: After I left him this evening,
I turned around for another glance or two. His
large, pale face in the window grew gloomier as
I walked away. His long eyelashes moved with
incredible slowness. A slim band of light suddenly
glowed from the lakeside and quivered over the
dark sky. I ran to see—

WOMAN IN NET:
Two human specks,
a mother and her child,
we glided through the world
for six whole years,
which were unto me
but a few days,
and we were
a nursery rhyme,
threaded with tales
and miracles—

Until ever so lightly,
a breeze
a breath
a flutter
a zephyr
rustled
the leaves—

And sealed our fates:
you here,
he there,
over and done with,
shattered
to pieces.

TOWN CHRONICLER: Now she notices me and falls silent. The entire pier lies between us, but she reaches out as though I were standing right beside her.

WOMAN IN NET:
I was cut
with scissors
from the picture,
solitary ice
of absence
came to singe
my limbs.
I was touched,
I was blighted
by the frost
of randomness.

TOWN CHRONICLER: She forcibly shuts her mouth with both hands. Her great black eyes fill with terror. If you ask me, Your Highness, the poor woman has not the slightest comprehension of the words that leave her lips! Incidentally, I think she truly believes that if I only came and touched her, this false spell would be lifted. But it has been almost thirteen years since I touched another

person. Now I must hurry, Your Honor: it is
almost midnight, and I cannot be late for my
wife.

TOWN CHRONICLER'S WIFE:
A clear corpuscle, *minute spec*
glowed inside me, a golden
granule gleamed. I knew that
it was me, my soul,
my core, it was the purpose
of my being. Born
with me, I thought, and so
would die with me—
I did not know that I might live
long after it, that I would be
diaspora,
deciduous. *ephemeral/lasting short time*
A liar, too—
the kind who easily,
no eyelid batted,
dared to speak of:
me.

WOMAN WHO STAYED AT HOME:
I sank my teeth
into my flesh. I did not

go. I dwindled
like a candle.
Only he still lay
awake in me: now seeing,
now remembering, now crossing
through a hell. Now quiet
with his son. Or
laughing. Tasting
crumbs of happiness
with him—

Do not breathe,
or think
of what he sees, what he recalls,
what ails
his heart—wounded inside him.
Inside me
an extinguished eye lit up,
the eye of a half-devoured beast
in its predator's mouth.
What does he see
there, I asked, I screamed, I slammed
my head against the wall, and how
swept up, how peeled away, and how
far has he gone
toward the darkness?

WALKING MAN:
I seem to understand
only things
inside time. People,
for example, or thoughts, or sorrow,
joy, horses, dogs,
words, love. Things that grow
old, that renew,
that change. The way I miss you
is trapped in time as well. Grief
ages with the years, and there are days
when it is new, fresh.
So, too, the fury at all that was robbed
from you. But you are
no longer.
You are outside
of time.
How can I explain
to you, for even the reason is
captured in time. A man from far away
once told me that in his language
they say of one who dies in war,
he "fell."
And that is you: fallen
out of time,
while the time

in which I abide
passes you by:
a figure
on a pier,
alone,
on a night
whose blackness
has seeped wholly out.
I see you
but I do not touch.
I do not feel you
with my probes of time.

CENTAUR: Take you, for example, Town
Chronicler, or whatever it is you call yourself.
You're a real sight for sore eyes, you are. Get a
load of that bowler hat, boss! And the tie, and the
satchel, and the pencil mustache—*mwah*! It's just
a shame you look so bedraggled and filthy, like
some kind of tramp. And also—I'm sorry—but
you reek like a fresh pile of droppings. Other than
that, though—

    All right, all right, no need to get in a huff!
What are you talking about? Insulting a civil
servant? Hah! Lighten up, pencil pusher, I'm just
joking around. Besides, you should know that

it's all from jealousy. Yes, write that down in the
biggest letters you can make: *The centaur is jealous of
the clerk!*

No, you tell me: Isn't it incredibly fortunate
that you, as part of your job, and undoubtedly in
return for a handsome salary, can spend as much
time as you want peering into other people's hells,
without dipping so much as your pale little pinkie
inside them? Think about it! What could be more
titillating than someone else's hell? And besides,
I'm sure you'll agree that secondhand pain is
far better than firsthand. Healthier for the user
and also more "artistic" in the sublime—I mean,
the castrated—sense of the word. Take you, for
example: it's been at least a week now since you've
been coming here, just by chance, walking past
my window three or four times a day—yesterday it
was five, but who's counting—hurrying about your
business, lost in thought, when suddenly: *Bam!* A
screeching halt! A surprised blink! What do we
have here? Why, it's a centaur! And a bereaved
one, at that! Two for the price of one! I'd better
quickly put on an expression of tender sorrow
and commiseration, and in a flash I'll dip my
silver-plated quill in its black ink, and one-two-
three, I'll ask about the son, ask about the son,
ask about the son! And if the subject's answers

are not satisfactory, I won't give up, no, I won't
give up, I'll come back in an hour or two, and
tomorrow morning again, and I'll ask about the
son again, and I won't relent even if the subject
grits his teeth and bites his tongue until it hurts,
and please tell me what he was like as a baby,
what he liked to eat, what he built with Legos,
which lullabies you sang to him . . . Well, listen
up, you black-inked tick: even the inquisition's
tax assessors didn't torture people like this! And
then all of a sudden, *psshh*! The town clock strikes,
ding-dong, see you later, thank you very much, it's
been a pleasure, the quill goes back in its case,
the notebook in its folder, and the pencil pusher is
on his way home, open parenthesis, what does he
care that I'm sitting here bleeding, ripped apart,
slaughtered to pieces, close parenthesis, clerko
hums a happy tune and ponders the leg of lamb
waiting for him in the oven, and probably the legs
of some lady or other . . . What? Hey? Did I grab
you by the what's-it or didn't I?

TOWN CHRONICLER: Enough is enough, Your
Highness! I have reached the end of my tether!
From here on out, your town chronicler adamantly
refuses to meet with this despicable creature. You
may kill me, my lord, but *I shall not go back to him*!

WALKING MAN:
I heard the voice
of a woman
coming from the town:
That every man is
an island,
that you c-c-cannot
know
another
from within—

I persist in trying: I resuscitate,
awaken, endlessly clone
cells of yours that still
live in me, the final imprints
of being that have not yet
faded from the tips of my sensations—
the touch of your child-skin,
your voice still thin
and secretive, yet lashing out already
with a sharp salvo of irony, an impression
of your torso moving,
passing quickly,
sliding (how happy I was
when they said
you walked like me).

The corner of your mouth
tugs with a fragile flash
of doubt—
I continue, I preserve,
I treasure
and revive the child
you were, the man
you will not be.
You may laugh: What is this, Dad,
one-human-subject research?
I shrug my shoulders: No, it is a
life's
work.
Look, I suddenly exclaim,
I will create you,
or at least
one life-twitch
of you, and why not,
damn it, why
give up?
I've done it once before,
and now I want
you
so
much
more.

WOMAN WHO STAYED AT HOME:
I drew
all the blinds. I dimmed
all the lights. My skin grew covered
with wounds and blisters. Dark
silence, dark
silence, days
and nights I was
inside it, an overdue
embryo, ossified,
conceived by the tragedy
in its senescence.
Until I emerged
from my torpor, and a voice
was conjured up from deep
inside me: I am
losing
my son
once again.

TOWN CHRONICLER: Under a streetlamp that
glows with a yellowish light stands an elderly man
writing in chalk on the wall of a house. A white
halo of hair hovers around his head, his walrus
mustache is silver, and my soul alights when I
realize it is my teacher, my math teacher from
elementary school, a likable man who suffered

a tragedy years ago, I cannot recall what, and disappeared. I thought he was dead, yet here he is, in the middle of the night, standing by a wall befouled with lurid pictures, writing columns of numbers and exercises in tiny, neat handwriting. When he notices me he does not seem alarmed at all: on the contrary, he gives me a toothless grin, as though he has been expecting me for a long time, and gestures with his crooked finger for me to approach the wall.

ELDERLY MATH TEACHER:
Two plus two
equals four.
Repeat after me:
three plus three equals
six. Ten plus ten—twenty.
You're late again, my boy;
tomorrow you'll have to bring
your parents.

TOWN CHRONICLER: But sir, don't you remember me?

ELDERLY MATH TEACHER:
Excuse me, sir, excuse me.
The darkness, and my eyesight . . .

You are the town chronicler,
of course.
So: with regard to the question
that was posed, or about
to be posed,
I have so little to say,
and I myself
must wonder: after all,
for twenty-six years
this has been
the singular
greatest fact
of my life.
Yet surprisingly,
and embarrassingly,
I know nothing
about it.
"But what is it like?"
people ask,
and I, too, not infrequently,
ask myself:
Like a block of concrete?
An iron ingot?
An impassable dam?
Like basalt rock?
Or rather—like the layers
of an onion?

But no, I must apologize,
for it is none of those.
And do not think, sir,
that I am evading
the question:
I truly know nothing about it.
Just that it is here.
A fact. And heavily
it slumps
on all my days. And
sucks my life out.
And that is all.
Please forgive me,
more than that
I truly
do
not
know.

TOWN CHRONICLER: He turned his back on me
and resumed writing numbers on the wall in his
miniature handwriting. I stood watching him for
several more minutes, drawing strange comfort
from the ease and swiftness of his motions. Then
suddenly I remembered what it was that had
befallen him, amazed that I could have forgotten.
I almost went up to him and said: Sir, such and

such happened to me as well, and you never
taught me what to do.

MIDWIFE:
A b-b-baby, one baby,
were he to emerge
from a womb into
my w-w-waiting hands,
my empty midwife's
hands, still c-c-covered
with the dew of birth, still tied
at the navel, bleating—
except that
I do not know
whether at that moment
he might not c-c-crumble
in my hands
to dust—

But w-w-what
is that?
Your m-m-mouth,
what have you
done?!

COBBLER: It's nothing. I don't—

MIDWIFE:
Your m-m-mouth,
the m-m-mouth,
open
your mouth!

COBBLER: No, leave it, don't touch, they give me
all my power.

MIDWIFE:
And I never
n-n-noticed . . . How?
I th-th-thought
it was only when you
worked that you . . . And how
did you eat that w-w-way?
How anything?
T-t-take them out, please,
I beg you, take them
all out—

COBBLER: No, I can't, who'll protect me so I—

MIDWIFE: *Take them out!*

COBBLER: So I don't bite me—

MIDWIFE:
Y-y-yes, more,
remove them, spit them, there are
more, and another,
yes, give them into my hand . . .
There are more, dear God,
it's sharp . . . there's blood,
your whole m-m-mouth
is sores and
rust.

TOWN CHRONICLER: She opens the window and
throws them out. I hear metallic clangs as they
fall around me. The cobbler stands there amazed,
his hand on his cheek and his tongue roaming his
mouth, probing the emptiness.

COBBLER: There were ten of 'em. The little ones
and the big ones and the crooked ones, and a thick
one with no head, what was like a thumb, I called
it. They've been like parts of me. One for each of
her tiny-tiny fingers I used to kiss.

TOWN CHRONICLER: That evening, the walking
man hears heavy footsteps behind him, and there
is the cobbler, slightly hunched, and he grunts
out a question: Happen to need some shoes? The

man says he doesn't need anything, only to walk
undisturbed. The cobbler looks at the man's
blistered feet and says he has, right there in his
backpack, tools and a stretch of leather, and he
can easily sew a fine pair of shoes. The man does
not reply, and they keep walking a while longer.
Finally, the cobbler asks if he may walk behind
the man this way, and the man doesn't answer,
nor does he stop walking, just shrugs his shoulders
as if to say: Do as you please, but I walk alone.

Now they are two, Your Highness. You can
see them from your window. At the fore, the tall,
thin man with unkempt hair and beard, and a few
steps behind him, the cobbler, his arms hanging
at his sides. Every so often he turns his head back
to see the slender, upright woman in the hut
window.

MIDWIFE:
But if
not,
if the b-b-baby does not
crumble to dust, if he stays
warm and s-s-solid,
wailing,
crying,
perhaps

the whole w-w-world
will return
to be mended
in my two hands?

WOMAN WHO LEFT HOME:
Five years after my son
died, his father
went out
to meet him.
I did not go
with him.
Atop a belfry
in the heart of the county seat
a hundred miles from home,
I walk alone now
in circles, around
a ferrous spire, slowly
slowly, around
and around, nights,
days,
in my tiny circle,
facing him,
while he
on the hilltops,
facing me, days,

nights,
orbits his
own circle.

CENTAUR: But if I don't write it I won't
understand.

TOWN CHRONICLER: This, as though in passing,
is what the centaur mutters at your chronicler,
my lord, as I walk past his window in the evening
hour—as I walk *at your command, and under profound
and turbulent protest.*

CENTAUR: I cannot understand this thing that
happened, nor can I fathom the person I am
now, after it happened. And what's worse, pencil
pusher, is that if I do not write it, I cannot
understand who *he* is now either—my son.

TOWN CHRONICLER: Nor do I understand what
he is saying. And he, of course, does not explain.
Only pricks up his nose in a proud and bombastic
display of insult and turns his back on me as far
as his ungainly body will allow. But he follows me
from the corner of his eye, and as soon as I grow
weary of his performance and turn to leave—

CENTAUR: That's how it is with me, clerko, that's how I'm built. No getting around it. I can't understand anything until I write it. Really understand, I mean. *Veritably!* What are you looking at? Again with that waif face? I'm talking about actually writing, not just regurgitating what a thousand people before me have chewed up and vomited, like you are so fond of doing, eh, keeper of the notebook? Snooping, snipping, jotting down every single fart with your precious handwriting, eh? Well then, write this, please, in big letters, giant ones: *I must re-create it in the form of a story!* Do you get that? *It,* you idiot! The thing that happened! What's not to understand? *It!* The sonofabitch thing that happened to me and my boy. Yes—mix it into a story is what I need to do, have to do. And it must have plots! And imagination! And hallucinations and freedom and dreams! Fire! A bubbling cauldron!

TOWN CHRONICLER: Large beads of sweat roll down the channels of his nose. His face is a crimson tempest. I feverishly write completely transfixed by him not looking at the page my hand rushing on its own

CENTAUR: That's the only way I can somehow get close to it, to that goddamn *it,* without it killing me, you know? I have to dance around in front of it, I have to move, not freeze like a mouse who sees a snake. I have to feel, even just for a minute, just half a second, the last free place I may still have inside me, the fraction of a spark that still somehow glows inside, which that lousy *it* couldn't extinguish. Ugh! I have no other way. You have to get that: *I have no other way.* And maybe there *is* no other way, huh? I don't know, and you wouldn't understand, so at least write it down, quick: I want to knead it—yes, *it,* the thing that happened, the thing that struck like lightning and burned everything I had, including the words, goddamn it and its memory, the bastard burned the words that could have described it for me. And I have to mix it up with some part of me. I must, from deep inside me, and then exhale into it with my pathetic breath so I can try and make it a bit—how can I explain this to you—a bit mine, mine . . . Because a part of me, of mine, already belongs to it, deep inside it, in its damn prison, so there might be an opening, we might be able to haggle . . . What? Write it down, you criminal! Don't stop writing. You stand there staring at me?

Now that I've finally managed to get out a single
word about it, and breathe . . . I have to create
characters. That's what I want, what I need. I
must, it's always like that with me. Characters
that flow into the story, swarm it, that can maybe
air out my cell a little and surprise it—and me.
Yes, I want them to betray me, betray *it*, the
motherfucker. I want them to jump it from this
side and the other and from every direction and
back to front and upside down, let them ram it up
the ass for all I care, just as long as they make it
budge even one millimeter, that's enough, so that
at least it moves a little on my page, so it twitches,
and just
makes it not
so
so impossible
to

anything.

TOWN CHRONICLER: He stops. There is terror
in his eyes, as though the ground is falling away
beneath his feet and he is plunging down as I
watch. He lifts one arm feebly, as if to grab me.
Only now, Your Highness, do I begin to grasp
what has been right in front of my eyes this whole

time: the notebook, the pens on the desk, the empty pages—

I stare at the bulky, crude creature. This was not something I had ever imagined.

CENTAUR: Now get out of here. I beg you, leave. But come back, yes? You'll come back? When? Tomorrow?

TOWN CHRONICLER: The next day, in a dusty drawer in the town archives, I locate his file. He was not lying: until a few years ago, he used to write stories. Poems, too, and ballads and one epic. I noticed that the experts generally wrinkled their noses, although he did garner the occasional accolade: "As with the biblical Joseph," one critic rhapsodized, "lust erupts from his fingertips."

The rumors circulating about him, and about his peculiar nickname, are also in his file. All sorts of tall tales, Your Highness, which I simply shudder to hear! I am almost tempted to write them down for amusement's sake, but when I encounter the sardonic look emanating from your portrait on the royal edict in my hand, I know I could never embarrass you by quoting such primitive nonsense in an official document of the duchy.

WOMAN ATOP THE BELFRY:
Sometimes people
climb the tower, tourists or
bird-watchers or bell lovers,
and mostly, those who come to watch
our war, waged eternally
in the valley beyond the hills.
They stand for hours, drinking, spitting,
looking through binoculars, gambling
on the results. They drink again, and scream
hurrah at the top of their lungs if
a soldier down there, some poor man—
too far
to tell
if ours or theirs—
manages with great effort
to raise his sword.
You were there, too,
my son. What
did you do there,
why would you
be there?
Between their hurrahs,
the drinks and the winks, they look
at me, point fingers, laugh,
sometimes pinch.
What do they see? A woman

from the village, from by the swamps,
with a village face and heavyset legs,
a long silver braid, barely moving, walking
slowly,
slowly,
three or four steps
an hour, a madwoman.
They can laugh.
Laugh all they want. I walk
around the spire slowly, one step,
another, and another step. My eyes
on him alone,
on the hilltops,
with them around me, and he
and I,
and me
and him,
and our
son
strung
between us.

WALKING MAN:
A ray reaches out from me
into me, touches
cracks and niches,
tenses:

Where are you?
On which of all the roads
will you reveal yourself,
in which of my orbs be divined?

A soccer game?
Making sauce for a steak?
Doing your homework,
head in hand?
Skipping pebbles
across the water?

I have known for a long time:
it is you
who decides
how to appear in me
and when. You,
not I, who chooses
how to speak
to me. But your vocabulary,
my son—I sense it—
diminishes as
the years go by.
Or at least does not
evolve: soccer,
steak, homework, pebbles.

You had so much more
(all your life, my precious, a vast array),
yet you seem to insist,
entrench yourself
in diminishment:
steak, ball, pebbles, homework,
another two or three
small moments to which you turn,
return.
Dawn on a riverbed, up north,
the story I read to you there,
the alcove in the strange gray
rock in which you nested,
curled.
You were
so small,
and the blue of your eyes,
and the sun, and the minnows
that leaped in the water as though they, too,
wished to hear the story, and the laughter
we laughed together.
Just that, just those, again
and again,
those memories, and
the others
gradually fade . . .

Tell me, are you purposely
robbing me
of solace?

And then I think, Perhaps
this is how you slowly habituate
me to the ebbing
of pain? Perhaps,
with remarkable tenderness,
with your persistent
wisdom,
you are preparing me
slowly
for it—
I mean,
for the separation?

CENTAUR: You're back. Finally. I was beginning
to think you'd never . . . that I'd scared you off.
Look, I was thinking: You and I, we're an odd
couple, aren't we? Think about it: I've been
unable to write for years, haven't produced even
one word, and you—it turns out—can write, or
rather transcribe, as much as you feel like. Whole
notebooks, scrolls! But only what other people
tell you, apparently. Only quotes, right? Other
people's chewed-up cud. All you do is jot it down

with a pen stroke here, a scribble there ... Am I
right? Not even a single word that's really yours?
Yeah? Not even one letter? That's what I thought.
What can I say, we're quite a pair. Write this
down then, please. Quickly, before it gets away:
And inside my head there's a constant war comma the wasps
keep humming colon what good would it do if you wrote
question mark what would you add
to the world if you imagined question
mark and if you really
must comma then just write
facts comma what
else is there to say
question mark write them
down and shut up
forever colon at
such and such time comma in
this and that place comma my son
comma my only child comma aged
eleven and a half
period the boy
is gone
period

TOWN CHRONICLER: And with these last words,
using both hands and terrible force, he pounded
the table, and his face contorted so painfully that

for a moment I thought, Your Highness, that he
had struck his own body.

MIDWIFE:
Dear God, such pain
cuts suddenly deep down
in my stomach, my girl—
if only I knew that *th-th-there,* too,
when you arrived,
when you finished
dying,
you were welcomed with loving arms
and a warm, fragrant t-t-towel,
and someone,
or something, in whose bosom
you found peace
in those first moments.

TOWN CHRONICLER: Next to the train station,
in the dark, by a lopsided house, stands the
elderly teacher. His silver head leans in against
the wall of the house to whisper a secret. With
a commanding gesture, as though once again
having been waiting for me, he invites me to sit
on the sidewalk by his feet. Two plus two equals
four, I murmur after him, and instantly feel relief.
Three plus three is six. Four plus four—eight. My

presence seems to fill him with life: he scribbles
exercises on the wall, his eyes aglimmer. Five plus
five is ten, I sing along joyfully, craning my neck
back to see him standing over me. His coattails
fly as he leaps from one exercise to the next. My
voice grows soft and thin. I imagine that my feet
do not reach the road and I can swing them. Ten
plus ten twenty, I cheer, and from the second-
story window someone empties a chamber pot of
wastewater on us and yells: People are trying to
sleep!

    I get up and stand next to the teacher. We are
both wet and shamefaced, as though caught in a
foolish prison escape. The teacher looks suddenly
small and shriveled like a baby. If only I could
touch, I would take him in my arms and rock
him and hum until he fell asleep. Instead I open
my notebook, and in the most official voice I can
muster, I ask him for details.

ELDERLY MATH TEACHER:
The questioners persist:
And has it no fissures?
No cracks
or crevices?

No.

And can you
touch it?

It has no touch.

But tell us: Is it full or
hollow, this great fact
of your life? Is it slack
or taut?

No, no,
I respond awkwardly, it's
here, it's
here!

But you've already said that!

Yes, it's odd how little
I have to say
on the matter. Surprising
and disappointing, I know,
but it, namely *that,*
meaning the death
of my son, of Michael,
twenty-six years ago
in a foolish accident
(a prank gone awry,

a bathtub, a razor,
veins slashed
in the course of a game),
it seemingly swallows up
the words and the wisdom,
all the keys.
Only one thing remains
steadfast:
it is here.

Whether I come or go,
whether rise or lie—
it is here.
When I am alone
or sitting in the square,
or teaching a class—
it is here,
filling me up entirely
until nothing is left and
there is no room,
sometimes, for myself.
Yes, that is certainly something I wanted
to say (and perhaps it should be noted):
that I have no room
for myself. Or just
for a breath. Yes,
that's the thing:

one
good
breath,
a deep
breath,
whole
and pure,
without the convulsion
of horror
in its depths—

But of the thing itself
(as I have said)—
nothing,
not one word.

WALKING MAN:
When I have a flash of memory—
you sitting over your homework in the kitchen,
or smiling on the beach, in an old photograph,
or just asleep in bed—
I instantly awaken
what came the moment before.
Or what will come the moment after.
Before my memory caught you;
after the photographer froze you.

Then I knead you:
so your features broaden
into a smile,
then slowly focus
in contemplation.
So your eyes light up suddenly,
change colors
in the light,
brim with fury
or amazement
or intrigue.
Thus you shall walk in your room,
this way and that, in the cool of the day,
small waves
of grace,
naïveté and youth
move beneath your skin,
your fair hair skips
on your forehead.
And now you will turn to me and say:
But, Dad, you don't understand—

Or in your sleep, beneath a sheet,
your chest will rise and fall,
rise,
and fall,

and rise again.
(Ah,
I have asked too much.
I will be punished.)
And yet,
my son,
you do move,
you do move
in me.

CENTAUR:
Sometimes I play games
on it, the goddamn *it,*
activities: "Death is
deathful." I wink at it,
like it's a little game
we play: "Death will deathify,
or is it deathened? Deatherized?
Deathered?" I patiently recite,
Over and over, rephrasing, finessing:
"We were deathened, you will be
deatherized, they will be
deathed."
What else can I do—
neither write
nor live. At least
language

remains, at least
it is still
somewhat free,
unraveled.

TOWN CHRONICLER: Tell me about the cradle.

CENTAUR: What's that? *What did you say?*

TOWN CHRONICLER: The cradle. In the big pile,
behind you.

CENTAUR: I hope with all my heart, you miserable
clerk, that my ears deceive me.

TOWN CHRONICLER: It has two ducks painted on
the side.

CENTAUR: It's a real shame, clerk. You've ruined
the moment.

TOWN CHRONICLER: His shoulders start to
swell. His cheeks, too. My gamble has failed. He
struggles to move himself away from the desk
and stand up. I have to get out of here, quickly.
I've never seen him not behind his desk. In fact,
until this moment I have not seen him stand. I

remember what I read about him in the town
archives. This is the time to flee, but my legs
disobey me. He grows larger and larger in front
of me. He will get up, that is clear, get up and
uproot the house with him and split the roof.
The toys and the clothes and the other remnants
of childhood will crumble to dust and scatter
every which way. It's a shame. Such a shame. I
was almost beginning to like him. He groans; his
face trembles. I hear, from there inside with him,
in the room, loud taps and a strange creak, like a
large, sharp fingernail scratching a tile. I close my
eyes and tell myself it's only the desk; it's just the
desk making that sound. A thought flies through
my mind: He will get up from his chair and pluck
me into his room and devour me. And another
thought: That desk has hooves.

CENTAUR: Damn, damn! Not even stand up? Shit.
Shit!

TOWN CHRONICLER: His head plunges onto his
chest and he weeps. I swear, he weeps. I'd best be
gone. Otherwise I will embarrass him. I will wait
one more moment and then leave. His shoulders
heave. Quick, truncated shudders. He covers
his face with his hands. I count the cracks and

grooves in the sidewalk. Correct a few mistakes in
the notebook. Then, having no choice, I begin to
listen to the different layers of his sobbing until I
hear one I know well. If I were to cry, this is likely
how I would cry. I listen. From the minute the
thing happened to my daughter, I forbade myself
any self-pity whatsoever. This requires, of course,
a certain degree of self-control and constant
guardedness. At night, too. I cannot forbid the
centaur to cry, however. That is his private affair,
even if for some reason he insists on weeping in
my voice. I try to guess what my wife would do in
this situation. I rise up on my tiptoes. My hand
hovers over his head. This is a hand that has no
right to touch a person. Pathetic, impure, the
hand of a coward. I take a deep breath and shut
my eyes and caress his curls. "There, there," I say.

He falls silent. Silence descends on the whole
town. I dare not move. Thus, with my hand
resting on the centaur's head, I suddenly hear,
very close, right in the place where my hand
touches the large, sweaty head, the voice of the
man who walks the hills.

WALKING MAN:
In the first year
after, alone at home,

I sometimes called your name,
your childhood
nickname.

With strength I did not possess,
in madness, with dauntless
peril to body and soul,
I would imbue that short,
yearned-for
word
with magic dust:
domesticity,
serenity,
routine.

Then utter a calculated, casual:
"Uwi?"

If I said it just right, I hoped
(I dreamed, I schemed),
you could not refrain
from responding
to the simplicity,
which transcends
worlds and borders—

I would say "Uwi" and you would
slide down and come true
in a blink, the echo
of my call,
a minor tide
trickling from the there
into the here. And that would be
your answer,
natural and practical,
as exhalation
answers inhalation,
a tribute
to the miracle of
powerful routine.

Oh, I would say to you,
watch a game with me? Or
shall we take a walk
together now?

How did it happen, my child,
that of all my words,
there is one
that will never,
ever
be answered?

TOWN CHRONICLER: "But where is *there*?" asks my
wife the next day as we take our evening walk—
she down the street, me following her, hidden by
the shadows. "Where is this *there* he's going to?
Who even believes that such a place exists?"

As she ambles, she throws these words into the
air. I feel almost weak-kneed from the surprise.
I look around to see if anyone has heard her, but
fortunately it is only she and I on the street at this
hour.

"Maybe *there* has been here all this time?" she
continues, and the matter-of-fact cadence of her
voice unsettles me even more: she might as well be
conversing casually in our kitchen.

"And maybe we've been there, too, just a bit,
since it happened to us?" She straightens up and a
new momentum seems to drive her steps. "Maybe
there has always been here, and we just didn't
know it?"

A cool breeze blows. She wraps a scarf around
her neck, leaving her beautiful shoulders bare.
She does that for me. Today is my birthday, Your
Highness, and she knows how much I love her
shoulders.

"And if that is the case"—she takes a deep
breath—"then maybe, maybe *she* is here with us,
every single moment?"

The powerful stab of the words makes us both
stop.
"Just imagine," she whispers.
We keep walking. She up front, I in the
shadows of houses and through darkened yards,
shaken.

ELDERLY MATH TEACHER:
"A father should not outlive his child."
The clear-eyed logic of this rule
is rooted not only
in human life, but also,
as we know,
in the science of optics, where
(in the spirit of the great Spinoza,
the lens grinder)
we find an extremely daring
axiom: *"The object*
('the life of the son')
must never be located
in the universe
at a distance
from which the father
('the observing subject')
may encompass all of him
with one gaze
from beginning to end."

For otherwise
(and here I interject),
the observing subject
would become
at once
a lump
of lignite
(known also as:
coal).

TOWN CHRONICLER: Now, from day to day, the
wayfarer's walk grows more vigorous. At times
it seems, Your Highness, that a nameless power
hovers over the town, envelops it, and—like a
person sucking an egg through a hole in the
shell—it draws these people and others toward it,
from kitchens and squares and wharves and beds.
(And—if there is truth to the shocking, dizzying
rumors, Your Highness—even from palace
rooms?)

The woman atop the belfry—once in a while
I look up and see her there among the clouds,
her silver hair unbraided, flying—she, too, must
sometimes cling to the spire with both arms or
else be swept up in the invisible storm. Now, for
instance, her mouth is agape, and I do not know

whether she is shouting out in the silence or
eagerly swallowing words as they float past.

WALKING MAN:
Like a fetus hatching
from its mother's womb and body,
his death made me the father
I had never been—
it bored
a hole in me, a wound,
a space, but also filled me
with his ubiety,
which churns in me now
with an affluence
of being I have never
felt before.
His death
has qualified me
to conceive him.

His death
makes me
an empty slough
of father—and of
mother: it bares
my breast for

no one there to suckle.
And on the walls
of my womb,
which on that day was hewn,
his death—with fleeing captive's fingernails—
notches off the score of days
without him.

Thus, with lucent chisel,
his death
engraves its news on me:
the bereaved
will always
woman be.

TOWN CHRONICLER: The next night, my wife
and I take our daily walk again. Between the
houses we catch an occasional glimpse of the
small procession ambling over the hilltops on the
horizon.

TOWN CHRONICLER'S WIFE: In recent days I
think I see, over their heads, in the air, some sort
of reddish flicker, a chain of embers hovering
above . . .

TOWN CHRONICLER: As usual, she sets our pace. When she pauses, I stop, too. Sometimes, when she is lost in thought, I must enter a yard and huddle behind a fence, praying I won't encounter a dog. At this moment she watches the strange embers at length, and I, as always, watch her. The faint moonlight falls on her face. She was so beautiful once. She is now, too.

When we finally arrive at her home, she opens the door. But tonight she lingers at the doorway, turns, and looks straight into the dark, as though guessing exactly where I am hiding. I feel the home current wafting toward me, warm and fragrant. She hugs her body and sighs softly. I may be wrong, but perhaps it is her way of telling me that she would like to fall upon me now, screaming, teeth bared, and beat me furiously with her fists, tear my skin off with her nails.

She slowly shuts the door. Retreats into her home. I look up to the hills.

WALKING MAN:
And he himself,
he is dead,
I know now.
I now can say—though
always in a whisper—"The boy

is dead."
I understand, almost,
the meaning of the sounds:
the boy is dead. I recognize
these words as holding truth:
he is dead. I know.
Yes, I admit it: he is dead.
But his death—it swells,
abates,
fulminates.
Unquiet,
unquiet
is his death.
So unquiet.

ELDERLY MATH TEACHER: . . . Based on my
observations, I believe, my boy, that only a certain
type of person is likely to notice it—the *blaze*.
That, between me and myself, is what I call those
mysterious embers.

TOWN CHRONICLER: I met him again by chance
tonight, at three o'clock in the morning. This
time he was not writing exercises on the wall.
Tired, defeated almost, he sat down in the dark
on the street bench where I was napping. After
we shared a moment of embarrassment, and

after I reminded him that I had been his pupil
in the first grade, and that it was in his class that
I had met the woman who would eventually
become my wife, we climbed up onto the
bench together and stood there watching the
phenomenon.

ELDERLY MATH TEACHER: My heart tells me, my
boy, that from the moment a person notices the
blaze, he is destined to get up and go to it.

TOWN CHRONICLER: As he spoke, his large feet
shuddered and shook the wooden bench. My own
small feet were suddenly filled with motion. I
talked to him silently. I said there was a time in
the world when my daughter was not in it at all.
She was not yet. Nor was there the happiness she
brought me, nor all these torments. I wanted him
to look at me with his lost, confused gaze in which
everything was possible. I wanted him to call me
to a house wall again and test me on addition-
subtraction for all eternity. I thought: Perhaps he
also longs to be an innocent young teacher again?
Perhaps I could ask my wife here, and together
we could build a little class that would suffer no
sorrow? I had already begun to hum "two and
two are four" when he suddenly leaped off the

bench—I was amazed to see how agile he still
was—and stood looking at his twitching feet.
Then he spread his hands before me in apology
and turned to leave, mumbling to himself:

ELDERLY MATH TEACHER:
Here I will fall,
now will I fall?
I do not fall.
Here is shadow
and fog,
frost
rises
from a darkened pit—
now,
now
I will fall—

TOWN CHRONICLER'S WIFE:
Now, here,
the heart
will stop—
it does not stop—
here is shadow
and fog—
now?
Now will I fall?

TOWN CHRONICLER: And she walked! Walked away! Suddenly, out of the darkness, she appeared beside me on the street, then walked away without seeing me at all, moving behind the teacher as if sleepwalking. I quickly lay down on the bench and made myself as small as possible. I was very cold. I tried to fall asleep. I could not. I do not know what I shall do with myself today, and the sun has not even risen. The town is terrifyingly empty. I wander the streets. No one. I run to the wharf, dig through reeking piles of nets and dry seaweed—no one. Where will I go? There, on the hilltops, the small embers glow tonight as though each holds a beating heart. In a dark yard at the edge of the market stands an old gray donkey eating from a trough. I hold my face up to its mane and rub my nose in it. To my surprise, it is soft, softer even than the centaur's hair. Perhaps things in the world have softened in my absence? The donkey stops chewing. He waits for me to talk. Of that thing that happened to her, to my daughter, I must never speak with any person—I explain to him—and if truth be told, I am forbidden even to mention her, although I don't always stick to that, particularly since that man began circling the town. The donkey turns his head to me. His gaze is wise and skeptical. It's

true, I whisper, I'm not allowed to remember her.
Just imagine! He twitches his ears in surprise. It
was the duke, I say as I throw my arms around
his neck. It was he who commanded me, in a royal
edict, to exile myself from my home, to walk the
streets day and night recording the townspeople's
stories of their children. And it was he who
forbade me—by explicit order!—to remember
her, my one. Yes, immediately after it happened,
he sentenced me, after she drowned, I mean the
daughter, Hanna, after she drowned in a lake
right before my eyes, and I couldn't, listen, there
were tall waves, huge, and I couldn't . . . What
could I . . .

You don't believe me. You're moving your ears
dubiously, even crossing them as if to dismiss
the possibility . . . I know exactly what you're
thinking: *The duke? Our kind and gentle duke? It cannot
be!* Everyone in town thinks so, and honestly,
sometimes I think so myself. Perhaps you've
heard that we used to be good friends, the duke
and I. Soul mates. Yes, after all, I was his jester
for twenty years, until the disaster befell me.
His beloved jester . . . And to think that he, of all
people, decreed such a terrible decree . . . How did
it even occur to him?

My lips suddenly quiver, and the donkey cocks

his head and studies them. I fear he might read
in them words I would rather keep to myself, or
those that I am forbidden by the edict to even
utter, or remember, even the slightest hint or
word or thought of the person she would be today,
if she were. I may not imagine her at all, nor
dream her image. Nor are longings, yearnings,
and so forth permitted. Or sudden heart pangs,
or churning contractions of the gut, nor any kind
of crying, whether sobbing or the faintest sleepy
whimper. A memory-amputee is what I am,
donkey. Abstaining from my daughter. A prisoner
in a tiny remote cell inside my spirit, until, as in
the poem we once read together, the duke and
I, *"My life (which liked the sun and the moon) resembles
something that has not occurred."*

COBBLER:
There is no longer anything in me
of myself that used to be.
Only motion remains.
That is all I can give you
today, my girl,
only motion
that might seep
into the stillness
where you lie.

Only that,
only thus will I know
today, my daughter,
how to be your father—

MIDWIFE:
I stood in the window
of my home, at night,
alone, slowly
diminishing.
As in a dream
I heard a distant
v-v-voice
speaking to me
in my tongue: *Only that,*
my daughter, only
thus will I know
today how to be
your father.
I knew: This was
the sign.
I left
my house,
turned
to the hills,
closed my eyes,
shut off my gaze,

allowed the blaze
to gather me in. *Only thus*
will I know today how
to be your father.
I hurried,
I ran to him,
to the heavy m-m-man,
so thick and slow,
who suddenly
spoke
in my tongue.

TOWN CHRONICLER: They walk on the hills and
I follow them, constantly darting between them
and the town. They groan and trip and stand,
hold on to each other, carry those who sleep,
falling asleep themselves. Nights, days, over and
over they circle the town, through rain and cold
and burning sun. Who knows how long they will
walk and what will happen when they are roused
from their madness? The duke, for example—
who would have believed it—walking shoulder to
shoulder with the net-mender, her fluttering nets
occasionally wrapping themselves around him.
And the elderly teacher, with his thin halo of hair,
walking swiftly, as he is wont, hopping from one
foot to the other and reaching his head out to

either side with immense curiosity, even in sleep.
And the cobbler and the midwife, hand in hand,
eyes tightly closed, with stubborn resolve. And
at the end of the small procession walks my wife,
dragging her heavy feet, her breath labored, her
head drooping on her chest, with no one to hold
her hand.

DUKE:
Walking half asleep,
a dream fragment flickers:
the surface of a barren wilderness,
mist and cool breeze, and a wail
rolls over
the desert.

MIDWIFE:
Over there
a c-c-cliff
c-c-cut into round
smooth rocky mountain,
and in a dream
or half awake, I say to myself:
L-l-look, woman,
that is the thing, that is all,
the answer to the great, sacred riddle,
and there is nothing

more,
there is
nothing more.

COBBLER:
Barren brain-hill,
a terrible sight,
it pulsates perhaps
once
in a thousand years—

TOWN CHRONICLER'S WIFE:
It is the brain of the universe,
and it is cold, frozen. It is not
what emits the wail. It is
desolation, only desolation,
mute and deaf
and flat,
it has no wails,
no thoughts,
it has
no answers and
no love.

DUKE:
And you—pick up
a hoe and till a bed.

Plant in it a pillow, a lamp,
a letter, a picture of
a beloved face, perhaps also a kettle,
thick socks, gloves and a satchel,
a pencil or paintbrush, a book
or two, a pair of glasses, so that you
can see near
and see far.

TOWN CHRONICLER: Tell me about the rocking
horse.

CENTAUR: You again? Won't you ever shut up?

TOWN CHRONICLER: Tell me about the soccer ball,
about the cowboy hat. About the birthdays, tell
me about them. About the magician's wand, the
blue kite—

CENTAUR: You're torturing me.

TOWN CHRONICLER: About the toy boat—

CENTAUR: Junk! Memory husks!

TOWN CHRONICLER: At least tell me something
about the cradle.

CENTAUR: How about you tell me something about yourself for a change? You've been coming here for weeks, ten times a day, interrogating me, turning me inside out like a glove, and you yourself—nothing! Just a clerk! Following orders! Hiding behind your royal edict, which any idiot can see is a fake, with that ridiculous drawing of the duke wearing a crown. I mean, come on! You could have put a little more effort into it. A five-year-old can draw better than that!

Okay. I get it. I can be quiet, too. Here. Being quiet. A rock. A sphinx. You're not looking so hot yourself either, you know, these last few days, but I am absolutely going off the deep end, yes, that's not hard to see. This fight with *it*, goddamn it, is doing me in. I admit it. And this silly thing that happened to me with the desk? I bet you've heard the stories around town, right? For that reason alone you should have stopped bothering me with your nonsense. Don't you have any mercy for a poor centaur? And a bereaved one, at that? Come on, look at me. No, I mean it. Climb up on this window, use both hands, don't be afraid. What's the worst thing I could do to you that you're not already doing to yourself?

So? Nice, isn't it? Aesthetically pleasing. Have you ever seen such grafting? Such a curse? Half

writer, half desk? Well, there you have it. You can
get down now. *Finita la tragedia*. What do you say?
It's quite a thing, isn't it? Didn't I tell you there
was nothing as pleasurable as other people's hell?

TOWN CHRONICLER: Your son once lay in that
cradle.

CENTAUR: And now he has a different one.

TOWN CHRONICLER: Help me, Centaur. Those
piles of yours are driving me mad.

CENTAUR: I'll never leave this place.

TOWN CHRONICLER: Thirteen years ago I lost my
daughter.

CENTAUR: These last few days, when you were
being a real pain in the ass, I was beginning to
think it might be something like that.

TOWN CHRONICLER: I can't talk about her.

CENTAUR:
I built the cradle
with my own two hands. The day

he was born, from branches of oak. My wife
painted the two ducks.
She painted so beautifully.
She was a quiet,
gentle woman. She left me,
three years after
the boy did. If I could have,
I would have left me, too.
Adam—that was his name.
Adam. I placed him
in the cradle
after he was born. He lay there
with his eyes open, looked
at me, studied me with his gaze.
He was so serious! He always was,
his whole life. His whole
short life. Serious
and slightly lonely. Hardly
any friends. He liked stories.
We used to put on plays,
he and I,
with costumes and masks. You asked
about the cradle. My wife padded it
with soft fabric,
but he could only fall asleep
with me, on my chest. He would cling
to me.

I just remembered, you'll laugh,
but there was a special sound
I used to make to put him
to sleep on me. A sort of quiet,
deep, trembling
moan. *Hmmmm* . . .
Hmmmm . . .

TOWN CHRONICLER: Excuse me, sir, would you
mind if I also . . .

CENTAUR: Not at all . . . *Hmmm* . . .

TOWN CHRONICLER: *Hmmm* . . .

CENTAUR and TOWN CHRONICLER: *Hmmm* . . .

WALKING MAN:
Walking, walking,
neither awake nor
asleep, walking
and emptying
all my thoughts,
my passions,
my sadness, my fervor,
my secrets, my volition,

anything that is me.
Look at me, my son:
here I am not.
I am but a platform of life,
calling you to come
and be through me—
to occur, if only for a moment,
to once again be purified
by what is.
Come, do not hesitate,
be now,
I am gone,
the house is yours,
and it is furnished with every limb.
Flow into it, pool in it,
this blood is your blood now, the muscles,
your muscles. Come,
be present,
reach your arms
from world-end to -end,
rejoice from my throat, laugh, vibrate,
celebrate,
all is possible at this moment,
everything now is *yes,*
so love and burn and lust
and fuck.

My five hungry senses
are at your command like
five horses foaming at the mouth,
stomping, raring
to gallop to your never-end.
Do not stop, my boy,
your time is short, meted out,
my eyelids are trembling now,
soon I will come home,
soon my pupils will contract
in the light of confining logic. Quick,
taste it all, devour, be deep,
be sad,
determined, delighted, roar,
tremble with pleasure and power,
my pleasure is yours, my power, too—
enchant, shower your soul,
be the swing of a sower,
a cascade of grain and
golden coins streaming
like light—
be engorged like an udder,
and torrid as midday,
and rage, and rave,
tighten your hand into a fist until
arteries swell in your neck,

and be thrilled, like a heart, like a girl,
be agape, thin-skinned, alight
with the glory of
one-off wonders,
be a whole,
momentary fraction
of eternity.
And as you do so, pause suddenly, breathe, inhale,
   feel the air burn your lungs, lick your upper lip,
   taste the salt of healthy sweat, the tingle of life,
   and now say fully: *I*—
(Damn it, I realize now:
that pronoun is also
lost, it died
with you, leaving me
with only *he* and *you*
and *us,* and no one
will ever again
say *I*
in your voice.
That too. That, too.)
Just hurry, my boy,
dawn is rising, the magic
soon will melt, so you must love,
and, even if betrayed,
even if you taste the venom

of disdain, love
and be brave, but be cowardly, too,
be everything, touch defeat,
touch failure, hurt someone,
disappoint
and lie.
Quick, my boy, pass through all these,
there is no time to linger,
such illusions are so brief,
but you must touch, caress
a warm body, a woman,
bounteous breasts in your hands,
the head of a newborn child, unborn
to you.
Quick, quick, the first strip
of light—
see the world you never saw: New York,
Paris, Shanghai, so many faces
in this living
world—

No, no, stop—
it's too late now,
come back
to rest,
quick,
to obscurity,

to oblivion,
just do not see
with my own eyes
what happened
to you.

WALKERS:
Our feet
lift slowly
from the earth lightly
lightly we hover
between here and there
between lucidity
and sleep
the thread will soon
unravel
and we will glide
and look
at whatever is there
at whatever we dare
to see
only when walking
in a dream

TOWN CHRONICLER: Sleeping . . . They've been
sleeping almost constantly for days, sleeping their
minds away. Sleeping and walking, speaking to
one another in their dream, each head leaning
on another walker's shoulder. I do not know
who carries whom and what force drives them to
walk—

DUKE:
Sometimes, alone
in my private chamber,
I take off both shoes and look
at my feet and think
it is
him.

ELDERLY MATH TEACHER:
I hit him. He was
a stubborn boy, and impudent,
with strange opinions
even as a child, and I—spare
the rod, spoil the child—I had to
beat him.
When he raised his hands to protect
his face, I hit him
in the stomach.

WALKING MAN:
But where are you, what are you,
just tell me that, my son.
I ask simply:
Where are you?
Ayeka?
Or like a pupil before his master
(for that is how I often see
you now),
please teach me—as I not long ago
taught you—
the world and all its secrets.
Forgive me if my question
sounds foolish and insipid, but
I must ask because
it has been eating
at my soul like a disease
these past five years:
What is death, my son?
What
is death?

MIDWIFE:
Great, definitive death,
my girl,
with b-b-boundless power. Eternal,

immortal d-d-death. And yours.
Your single, little death,
inside it.

COBBLER:
Actually, I wanted
to ask, What's it like,
my girl, when you die?
And how are you
there?
And who are you
there?

DUKE:
It is a perplexing thought, my son,
but perhaps you now know
far more than I do?
Perhaps a new and wondrous world
now carries you in flight,
and with a massive flap of wings
it spreads out
its infinity, just as
in our world here it long ago
lavished your soul with its abundance,
your pure, boyish soul. I feel
so young and ignorant before you.

TOWN CHRONICLER: Every so often a tremor
passes through them, all of them, one after the
other, as though an invisible hand had slid a caress
down the spine of the small procession, lingering
lightly over the head of each and every one. In
their sleep, they straighten up toward it like blind
chicks hearing their mother's voice, and their eyes
glow through their lids.

MIDWIFE:
I see her
jumping,
dancing in the kitchen,
before she fell ill,
when she still
had the strength. And her f-f-father,
my man, my love,
my cobbler, kneels before her
and places his hands: shoes for her feet.

COBBLER:
Am I dreaming?
I hear my wife.
I swear
her words are
hardly broken
anymore!

MIDWIFE:
. . . he walks her
through the house in his
hand-shoes, and laughs
until the roof almost flies off,
and she hugs his neck
and squeals, she has only just
learned how to talk,
you remember,
just beginning to say
her first words,
Dad-dy,
Mom-my,
Lil-li-li-li-Lilli.

COBBLER:
Lilli,
my
Lilli.

WALKERS:
We walk. Impossible
to stop. My body
won't allow it. My feet
are weak. And me, my breath
is short, yet still our body
will not stand. It pushes from inside, onward,

onward . . . It's like
going to meet your sweetheart,
isn't it, Mrs. Chronicler? Yes,
my lady of the nets, it's like a lovers' rendezvous.

WALKING MAN:
This void,
this absence,
death alone can render—
and it is not at all
a disappearance,
a cessation,
nothingness.
It has one final place,
a window opened
just a crack, where still
the absence breathes, still loosened,
palpitating, where one can still
touch the *here,*
still almost feel
the warming hand that touches
there.
It is the threshold,
one last line shared both by here
and there, the line to which
—no farther—
the living may draw near,

and where, perhaps, they still can sense
the very tip,
just one more hint,
the fading embers, slowly dying,
of the dead.

ELDERLY MATH TEACHER:
You have become your death
so much that sometimes I must wonder
(Forgive me, have I crossed a line?
Best to be quiet? To ask? You know,
my son, I am a gentlemen, yet find myself unsure
how to address you . . . May I use the second
    person?),
but tell me, speak it clearly,
show no pity:
if they were to allow you—*they,*
there—if you were given liberty
to choose—
would you come back?
Come back to this?
To me?

DUKE:
Or, as Rilke wrote of Eurydice,
are you, my child,
abundant with your own death,

which fills you
like a sweet and darkened fruit?
While I,
a bothersome Orpheus,
try to pull you
over here
against your will?

ELDERLY MATH TEACHER:
Just one more, if I may?
(Whom else can I ask
but you, my teacher
in these mysteries?)
Tell me just what is the thing
in us, the living,
whereby we can become
completely dead
within an instant,
in the blink of our own death?
And give up everything,
be given up on,
as though a primal law
that always lurked inside us
suddenly appears and rises
like a shadow from the depths: around it
still the ruins mount,
and comfortably it settles in,

a haughty landlord long in charge,
its stony glare—which does not miss
a thing, yet sees nothing—
declares with just
a hint of triumph
in its smile—
"Death, my friends, is what is true!"

WALKERS:
When we meet . . . What will we tell them
when we meet? I, gentlemen,
have already made up my mind:
I shall not tell him of his brother,
born after his time. In her room
we changed all the pictures.
We couldn't bear it any longer.
I ended up giving his dog
to a boy on the street.

(silence)

WALKING MAN:
And after some time,
whatever I do, you
fossilize.
Then I must
carve you,

time and again,
out of the layers of stone
in which you are
cast. I must try very hard
to want it—
must carve myself for it, too,
must fight—
while my whole being
shouts: Let go, it's best
this way. Let human nature
do as it will, you must
accept his fate, respect
his border—
But then I soon suspect
myself: perhaps deep down
I long for you
to fossilize?
To bleed no more.
To not be
so awake, so sharp,
white-hot and
everdead.

But no less painful
are the times when I succeed,
when my imagination
cleaves the hunk of stone until

it cracks, then crumbles,
falls around you,
and then suddenly
you are there:
naked,
breathtaking,
glowing in the palm of rock,
or merely standing,
limp
and incidental,
you look this way
and that, embarrassed, without knowing
that I watch you: present,
so present,
neither promising nor
disappointing, only
coolly beating with the pulse
of your calm being.
Just warm
enough.
And living.
Maddening.

WALKERS:
When we meet, if
we meet,
what shall I tell him?

What shall I tell her?
Do you think they know?
Know what? That they
are dead.

DUKE:
In August he died, and
when that month was over, I wondered:
How can I move
to September
while he remains
in August?

WALKERS:
Perhaps we'll simply
face them, when we meet,
without a word? Perhaps
he'll say that now he understands
I only hit him
for his own good? I might sing her
the song I sang when she was
just a baby. I want to get there
soon, dear God. I'm afraid
he'll be a stranger
to me. Rock-a-bye, baby,
in the treetop, when the wind blows . . .
Just to be there

with her, just to be. I wish
I could take him
a bowl of tomato soup.

WALKING MAN: No, no . . . It can't be, it can't be—

WALKERS: *It can't be, it can't be—*

WALKING MAN: It can't be that it happened to me,
it can't be that these words are true—

WALKERS: *It can't be, it can't be—*

WOMAN IN NET: That I saw them throwing my
boy into a pit in the earth—

MIDWIFE: That I heard—*thud-thud-thud*—the sound
of a hoe digging in the soil—

WALKERS: *It cannot be that these words are true, they*
cannot be the truth—

WALKING MAN: It simply cannot be.

MIDWIFE: Burn! Burn the words! Burn this
miserable talk!

WALKERS:
We look up, we know
just where to look, to the fire,
the small fire,
the constant flame,
day and night it walks
with us, we're used to it.
I, my friends, call it: the blaze.
Forget it, those are just small embers,
not anymore, not anymore,
look at the fire, inside,
it's alive, it's like life—
Don't move, wait, don't anger it,
it's opening,
peculiar, now
stretching out, slowly
slowly reaching hands, arms,
my God, what is this,
fingers—

WOMAN IN NET: In the earth! The earth is where
his little body rots!

WALKERS:
The air trembled loudly, the arms
of fire bristled, froze briefly in a glowing,

burning crystal, then started once again
to spin, to flower in wild blossoms,
then up above exploded
in a rush of molten fire, waxed
and roiled, above our heads
the fingers spread, lines of fire
flooded, slashed through
shadows, images, and suddenly
like whips they lashed, leaped, caught—
caught whom—the words—
the words? The miserable words,
they devoured all the it-cannot-be,
they swallowed all of it in fire, everything
went up in flames, we shouted
bitterly, a black-and-yellow flame
shot up from deep inside us, then
we fled—
kept still—
we screamed—
we froze, while she—
her flames of lionesses,
dragons,
snakes, we promised
silence
yet we screamed, we vomited
a brew of words, horrendous
words, it cannot be,

it cannot be, *and she—*
keeps thickly rising, bustling,
rounds of fire chasing us, and
now inside us, eyes of red
and black, they open,
tracking us, tongues
burning, let her come and burn,
damn words, she blackened memories, and scenes
we have not dared to see for years, she ate them, gulped,
a huge fire, swallowing and scorching, lapping
in our gut,
we barked, we wailed
at the mad fire, take everything,
take all of it, burn it to ashes
while we suffocate in the smoke
of words, the furnace—

Weary,
empty, standing,
tripping, faces
blackened as she dies
down finally,
then silence,
silence, tiny flames
abating, sated,
shhhhh . . .
asleep

(pause)

What, what was that?
Was I dreaming? Sleeping?
Look at me! I'm breathing!
So light of limbs now suddenly, the body
floats on air . . . Tell me, madam, am I
dead? Alive?
Your face, my woman. Touch me,
touch. How strange,
it's smooth, just like
it was
before—

Want—
I want—
I
want, we want
to wake up,
to wake out
of it, to wake into the light, I want
to dip, to bathe my everything
in light—

You—
All of you—
Who cannot hear—who do

not answer—lying heavy
on our hearts—drawing
out our blood—sucking every drop
of life from us—collecting
tax—a coldness tax—
from every moment of our laughter—
light—forgetfulness—
distraction—you who whisper
back each word we say from here

And why?—Have you considered that?—Why did you
become dead?—How could you be
incautious?—You weren't careful like we were—
Why did you go and pick up that disease?
And war,
why did you go to war?—
And to the waves—
The razor—

And how is it that you
are dead, while we
managed to stay alive?—Have you ever wondered
what that means?—Perhaps it is not chance
that you are there while we are here?—
Might you have even done something that made you
be this w-w-way?—
You know what? We don't even want to trouble ourselves

with these thoughts!—We don't even want to
think of you!—We've thought of you
enough!—We've thought enough
of everything. Before it happened
I didn't even know there were
so many thoughts!—Ahh, how many
years, dear God—how many tears—
So take—take—take your bundled bones—
and get out—get out of our lives—
Do you hear? Our lives!—
You,
All of you there—
Die now!

WOMAN ATOP THE BELFRY:
Quiet
has come.
The distant town
slammed shut
at once.
As though
there, too,
they all stopped
breathing.

WALKING MAN: But who am I?

COBBLER: Who are you?

WALKING MAN: I think I was looking for something here.

WOMAN ATOP THE BELFRY:
He left
and he came back,
he searched their faces
for all
that had been lost.
He ran
and circled
them,
and suddenly—
he fell.

WALKING MAN: Who am I?

ELDERLY MATH TEACHER: Pardon me, sir, do you happen to recall who I am?

COBBLER: Ma'am, any chance you remember—

MIDWIFE: There was a baby, and another baby, and another . . . Did they all come out of me?

WOMAN IN NET: There was a house, there were clothes—

DUKE: I played with horses, cavaliers—

TOWN CHRONICLER'S WIFE: And you, sir, who are you?

TOWN CHRONICLER: Me? I don't . . . Excuse me, ma'am, I don't know me.

WALKING MAN: Who am I?

WOMAN ATOP THE BELFRY (singing softly):
When I tell you yes,
you will embrace
the no,
embrace
the empty
space of him,
his hollow
fullness—

(pause)

There you are no longer
alone,

no longer
alone,
and you are not
just one there, and
never will be
only
one—

(silence)

WALKING MAN:
There
I touch him?
His inner self?
His gulf?

WOMAN ATOP THE BELFRY:
And he,
he also
touches you
from there,
and his touch—

WALKING MAN:
No one
has ever touched me
in that way?

WOMAN IN NET:
Two human specks
a mother
and
her child—

WALKING MAN:
What more must I do? My legs
can hardly carry me, my life thread
becomes thinner, a moment more
and I'll be gone. And you were right,
my wife, righter than me—
there is no *there,* there is
no *there,*
and even if I walk
for all of time
I will not get there, not
alive. So many days
have passed
since I left home,
and all in vain, no purpose, but
the passion still remains inside me
like a curse,
walk onward,
walk—

WOMAN ATOP THE BELFRY:
How miserable to be
so right,
while you were wiser
and far bolder.
Get up,
go and be
like him as much as
one alive can be
like the dead—without dying.
Conceive him,
yet be your death, too,
almost.
Like him
be now, but only till
the shadow of his end
falls
on the shadow
of your being.
And there, my love,
among the shadows,
in the netherworld
of father-son,
there will come
peace—for him,
for you.

DUKE:
Listen to her, sir
(my subject,
though subjected now
to no one), listen:
faithful are the wounds
of she who loves. Do it, and if not—
then you have sealed my fate,
our fate,
and we are nothing—
all of us who walk—
but a ripple over death,
a feeble sign, unreadable,
in the dense rock, from which
a wise but uncourageous sculptor
carved the merest hint of us, courageous
but not genius, or genius but surely
not merciful.
Go,
upend time,
conceive him and then die
with him, and be reborn
out of his death.

WALKING MAN:
Only the passion remains
in me, like a curse,

a disease—
walk, walk more, and
more.
Perhaps at some last border
where my wisdom cannot reach,
I will set down
this heavy load and then
take one small step backward,
no more, one pace
across the world,
a concession,
a confession:
I am here,
he is
there,
and a timeless border
stands between us.
Thus to stand,
and then, slowly,
to know,
to fill with knowledge
as a wound fills up
with blood:
this is
to be
man.

WALKERS:
And at that moment,
with those words,
the world grew
dark: a shadow
struck us all.
A wall.
A wall stood in our way. A massive
wall of rock bisected,
cut the world
right through.
A wall. It wasn't here before,
it simply wasn't!
A thousand times we've circled
round the town,
up and down these hills
until we know each stone and crevice, and
suddenly—a wall.

Perhaps we did not notice?
Perhaps we passed it
in our sleep? It was not here,
it wasn't! Then how? Then what?
From the sky? Or sprouted
from the ground?
Now it's here, it's here,
and maybe—

Could it be? Possible? But no,
my friends, no, science won't allow
such an assumption! But perhaps
our longings will? Perhaps
despair allows it?

Coldness
suddenly spreads
through our limbs. A cool shadow
cast upon us, slashing our world
like an ax,
like then, yes,
like the moment
of disaster—

And he,
the one,
the walking one,
the lonely,
nears the wall.
One step and then another. Fearful,
feet defeated, walking yet recoiling,
a grasshopper
beside it.

WOMAN IN NET: Enough! I'm going back.

DUKE: But we're not there yet. And what if *there* is right here, now, my lady, just behind the wall?

WOMAN IN NET: You listen to me, m'lord: farther than this we won't make it alive.

DUKE: Please, don't go.

WOMAN IN NET: Just so I understand, m'lord— you asking me to stay?

DUKE: When you are here, I am not afraid.

WOMAN IN NET: Give me your hand, m'lord.

WALKERS:
And he, facing the wall,
head cocked, listening,
awaits an answer. Where,
where will he go, where will we go:
along the wall? Or just stand here
and wait?
For whom? For what?
And for how long?

And as it always is with him, we know,
the feet. A tremble rises

from the shins, the body
tenses, head slowly lifts up
and straightens, and he walks. He walks.
It's good. This way is good. And everything
comes back to life along with him, one foot
lifts up, then steps back down, a step
and one more step,
one more, he walks,
walks and steps, steps
and strikes, he walks
in place—
in place? Yes, treading
in one place, a step,
another, one more step,
his eyes upon the wall, walking
without walking, walking,
dreaming, walking
with himself, from himself
to himself—

WALKING MAN:
Here I will fall
now I will fall—
I do not fall.
Now, here,
the heart will stop—
it does not stop—

TOWN CHRONICLER:
Here is shadow
and fog,
frost
rising
from a dark pit.
Now,
now I will fall—

WALKERS:
He does
not fall
and does not
fail, he walks, before the wall
he walks, a step,
another, one more step,
an hour goes by, another hour, sun sets
sun rises, weakened limbs. The shadows
of our bodies swallowed up
into the darkness as we walk,
we all walk
there—

And sometimes it does seem
that there is something moving in the wall.
It breathes. We do not say
a word. More than anything

we fear
the hope. Of what awaits beyond the wall
we do not dare to think. At dawn,
and twilight, too, our bodies elongate,
we grow into extremely slender
giants, silhouettes. And sometimes
deep inside there floats a golden speck,
fading from one, skipping to the other,
and this we do not speak of either. We walk in gloom.
Across the way, on gnarled rock,
a spider spins a web, spreads out his taut,
clear net. Then he creates a recess
and he burrows deep inside it—

Our faces
are sealed, our feet
strike, hit the earth,
the earth is also a wall.
The sky above as well, perhaps.
Walk, walk more, constantly
walk so as not to be crushed
between the walls. One step,
another, another step, our bleary eyes
see only humps of rocky stone,
scabs of brown and gray, and
a thin spiderweb waving
in the breeze—

Sunset pours its light upon the wall.
It almost draws attention for a moment. That light
of golden-red. Warm, appeasing
light. Since the day my daughter drowned, I gather up
each moment of beauty and grace, for her.
And I,
my friends,
ever since,
have looked
at things of beauty twice.
Oh, m'lord, I swear,
I'm just like you, except that
I don't have the words you have
from education. But Lady of the Nets,
you move me so each time
you speak of your son. Well, m'lord,
that's because poems suddenly
tumble out my mouth. It is the same
with me, my lady: poetry
is the language
of my grief.

Look—
there—
one green leaf.
Wondrous how it managed to sprout

here and survive in the naked,
arid rock. A fly lands on the leaf,
cleans its body,
scrubs and polishes
translucent wings—

We walk, alert, watching
the fly like a riddle—
vibrant, full of life, of lust;
it hovers and then
lands again, playful,
it should be more careful near the web.
But no—
the fool has touched the spiderweb,
brushed it with its wing,
now lost.

Disaster here, we know, instantly
now, disaster, its cold fingers
on our lips.
We walk fast, we walk
hard, threads bind.
The fly struggles, tries to take flight,
buzzes so loudly the sky might tear,
and its mouth opens wide:
What are you trying to say?

And what is it you know now,
that you did not know
when you were spawned?

A day or two later
at dusk, half asleep,
we notice that our stride
has changed. We walk, we step
so quickly, our skin bristles, what is it?
The earth, it seems, is softer?
Opening up to furrows
and dimples? Our feet understand
before we do, as they strike the earth,
deepening, dust rises,
backs straighten, eyes glimmer—

Each of us kneels down
upon the earth, digs into it with
hands and feet, with nails. Digs
quickly, like an animal,
and it trembles at our touch. Our hands
suddenly light, supple, fingers knead,
whole bodies dig in dirt and dust.

TOWN CHRONICLER:
My wife,
she, too.

Her lovely shoulders
moved, hovered.
An agile shape
danced in her
sorrow-heavy body,
slipped away, like moth
from dusty lamp . . .
She stopped. Wiped her forehead
with her hand.
I took my life
in my hands and smiled.
She smiled back! Up and down
I wiggled both my brows.
She smiled some more!
I went back to digging.

WALKERS:
The earth arches, curves itself
toward us, as if having waited
for a long time to be dug,
dug like this, for people such as us
to dig through it—we have a use now.
We sense how much it wanted
to be wallowed in, rejoiced in, laughed into—
tears and blood and sweat
are all we've piled into it always. When—
tell me—when has

someone laughed
into the earth?

The shadow
of the wall grows
longer over us, its blackness sharp
and cool. Teeth of iron
plow us with their umbra.
Vigorously, we fall
into earth's lap, turn over
in her, inhale her warmth
and breath, and she—the mother
of all life, and so the mother
of all dead, she is bereaved-in-life,
warm and fluttering in our hands,
as though begging us to go on,
to dredge up from her womb
the sweet desires of youth entombed
in her, the sweetness
of childhood which, in her,
has turned
into dust.

CENTAUR:
Imprisoned
in my room,
on my cursed body-desk,

I finally have written. Like fingers
probing crumbled earth,
I wrote the story.

WALKERS:
As day fades,
we linger by the wall
among deep trenches:
scars that we inflicted on the earth.
From time to time
our trembling glances fall
into their depths,
but quickly
turn away.

And he, the walker, rises
from the dust and looks at us,
and now it seems, for the first time,
his eyes greet us with kind blue light.
He smiles warmly to us each, and also,
so it seems, to those
whom each of us carries inside.
Soundlessly, with lips alone,
he whispers: Thank you.
Then turns, removes his clothes,
and here now he is
naked. His body is

so white,
human.

And down he goes
into the pit
he dug, and lies
there on his back, and
puts his arms
along his sides, and shuts
his eyes.

We stand.
Time comes
and starts
to rush: the cobbler
and his midwife
help the teacher
to remove his shoes.
The woman in the nets
and her friend the duke,
hand in hand, fleet fingered—
she from within,
he from without—
untangle the shock
around her body.
The chronicler and his wife
quietly help each other

remove their torn clothes,
both excited,
agitated,
and suddenly
they look
so young.

Naked
we stand,
taking our leave
with a gaze. Each of us
alone again.
Each bent over
his crater,
each descending
to her grave.

Then,
like a predator,
fast and sharp,
the night
lunges.

CENTAUR:
Now at last I understand:
The father does not move
his child. I breathe life

not into my son.
It is myself whom I adjure,
with words,
with visions,
with the scarecrow figures
glued with straw
and mud, and with
a poor man's wisdom,
lest I cease and turn to stone.
Lest I cease and turn
to stone.

In the cold white space
between the words,
it is my spirit
that is felled.
I alone flutter like prey
caught in the jaws
of finality.

For myself,
for my own soul, I fight
against that which diminishes,
which decimates
and dulls.

My whole life
now,
my whole life
on the tip
of a pen.

WALKING MAN:
It was
silent.
I lay
yoked
by loneliness:
the dolor
of a man
in earth.
The quiet voices
of the night
rolled in from afar,
clouds blew toward me
heavy, low, hiding the sky
from my eyes. The walls
of the pit drew close, closed in.
The earth is learning—
I sensed—measuring,
gauging: how it might
ingest me.

TOWN CHRONICLER'S WIFE:
We will be punished. I shivered
from the cold and fear. I thought:
People must not do
this sort of thing. I thought
about my beloved jester,
so miserable as he lies near me
in this bed of earth. And all the while
I felt the blood, blood dripping from me,
flowing into soil, reaching
all the way to him, seeping through his veins,
then coming back to me and melding.
Now it is our blood, and it is *her* blood now,
and both of us
conceive her
once again
from blood and earth.
I became dizzy,
and drowsy, and suddenly
it seemed so light,
as if time had also
loosened its bite.
I breathed. I slowly,
slowly breathed. I hadn't
breathed like that since then.
I haven't ever breathed like this.
My insides were exhaled,

then drawn back to me
like a gentle dance—

WALKING MAN:
Then I awoke
from frenzied dreams
that I could not remember.
The sky turned
lucent, the wall
towered up to split it.
I could not hear
my earthen neighbors, did not know
if they were here or gone.
Though I was cold, my fingertips
smoldered and hummed:
I will not be—they pulsed. They murmured
in ten voices, a cheerful choir:
I will
not be.
One day,
I will not beeee!
And from within the will-not-be
there rose the flavor
of my being. I knew
how much
I had been,
while I was. I knew

down to my fingertips.
It was wonderful
to know, to remember:
how very much
I'd been,
and how
I would
not be.

TOWN CHRONICLER:
I hope I forget your name,
my girl, the music of your name
inside my mouth, the sweetness that would spread
throughout my body.
You were so small,
yet so much in you to forget,
and not to want a thing that was once
yours,
nor even you
yourself—

DUKE: Who is that? I think I recognized my
jester's voice.

TOWN CHRONICLER: Indeed, my lord. It is I, your
servant.

DUKE: My soul mate.

TOWN CHRONICLER: It's been a long time since those days.

DUKE: More than thirteen years since you imposed this terrible exile upon yourself. Now tell me about your daughter.

TOWN CHRONICLER: I cannot, Your Honor. The day disaster struck, you ordered me to forget her.

DUKE: My beloved friend, you know better than anyone that such an order could never have entered my mind. Tell me about her.

TOWN CHRONICLER: No, no, my lord, I cannot. Your order still stands!

DUKE: Then, jester, I order you: *Forget her to my ears!*

TOWN CHRONICLER:
I forget her fine short hair.
I forget her pink, translucent fingers.
I forget she was my delicate, delightful girl.
I forget the way she—

the way you would get angry if I forgot
to separate the omelet from the salad on your
    plate.
And when I bathed you,
you would cheer and slap the water with both
    hands,
and I would lift you out and wrap your body
in a soft towel and ask:
Who is this strange creature inside?

CENTAUR: My friend the chronicler talked and
talked. A wellspring of forgotten gleanings
erupted from him. From my window I looked out
on the horizon. Between two hills I saw the vast,
empty plain where the pits were dug. Fragmentary
droplets shone in the starlight. The many
branches of a single, giant tree swayed slowly in
the wind, as if to welcome or to bid farewell.

Then a shadow suddenly moved upon the
plain. It was a woman extracting herself from the
earth. She took a few slow, heavy steps. She stood
hugging herself. Her head was slightly lowered.

TOWN CHRONICLER'S WIFE:
Who will sustain her,
who will embrace,
if our two bodies

do not
envelop
her?

CENTAUR: She looked around, studied the wall
at length, then disappeared down into the earth,
into the neighboring trench. After a minute or
two I saw a notebook hurled out of it. It flew
through the air for a moment, its white pages
swelling and glimmering in the darkness, then
vanished.

WALKING MAN:
I thought about the earthly
beings next to me. I thought
about my son. The earth
grew warm under my body.
I spoke to him in my heart.
At least we parted without anger—
I told him—
and without resentment.
You loved us, and were loved,
and you knew that you were loved.
I asked if I could make one more request.
I'd like to learn to separate
memory from the pain. Or at least in part,
however much is possible, so that all the past

will not be drenched with so much pain.
You see, that way I can remember more of you:
I will not fear the scalding of memory.
I also said: I must separate
from you.
Do not misunderstand me
(I felt the stab of pain
pass through him
right in my own flesh)—separate
only enough to allow
my chest to broaden
into one whole breath.
I smiled, because I remembered
that was what the teacher asked for.
The ocean sky rustled,
and a smile seemed to open up
above me. Someone may have understood,
or felt me. I breathed in
the full night. The sky
no longer weighed on me,
nor did the earth,
nor me myself.
Nor you.

You—
where are
you?

TOWN CHRONICLER'S WIFE:
Perhaps I need no longer reach
the very end of ways,
the final destination?
Perhaps this walk itself is both
the answer and the question?
Perhaps there is no *there,*
my girl, perhaps, too, no more
you?
But as I lie here, in the belly
of the earth, my pains abate
for one brief moment
and I feel and know
how life and death themselves
reach equilibrium inside me,
blissfully attuned (oh, but how
can my lips utter such vile words?!),
until like night and day, or
like the day of equinox,
when winter meets its summer,
the two mingle inside me,
granting wisdom and precision,
for which I paid a heavy price:
your life—
no, no!
A bitter,
loathsome bargain,

yet still, my girl—
allow me to say this or else
go mad—now, for the first time,
I know not only what
death is,
but also what is life,
and more than that,
I see—

TOWN CHRONICLER:
—how life and death
stand face-to-face,
cooing at each other.
How they touch,
braided with each other
at their naked roots.
How constantly they pour
and empty each into the other—
like a couple, like
two lovers—
the sap of
their existence.

TOWN CHRONICLER'S WIFE:
As they commingle,
so two rivers flow
into my confluence.

I did not know, not this way,
that life in all its fullness
is lived only there,
in borderland.
It is as though I never yet
have lived, as though all things
that happened to me
never really were, until
you—

WALKERS:
Morning broke. Thin red
clouds sailed through the sky.
We slowly rose
out of the tombs,
stood nude
outside the wall.
And once again we thought
we saw it tremble,
a wave, transparent,
passing up and all along it.
We could not speak; our breath
stood still: a wall
of rock
yet also
so alive.

MIDWIFE:
A face—

TOWN CHRONICLER'S WIFE:
There
in the wall,
in the stones,
I see
a face—

TOWN CHRONICLER:
No, my dear,
look here, at me. Here
is the face,
the warm, living body,
while there—
just a mirage
begat by yearnings.

TOWN CHRONICLER'S WIFE:
The face
of a young woman,
or a man,
or a boy—

DUKE:
And it moves
and it's
supple
and alive.

MIDWIFE:
I must be dreaming, certainly.
My God, is that a young man?
Or a boy?
Perhaps a *girl*?
Girl, g-g-girl,
please look
at me . . .

COBBLER:
They are
imprinted
softly,
as in beeswax
or on leather—

ELDERLY MATH TEACHER:
Or in reverie?
Or in a dream? No,
no, I am not wrong:

it is a human face
I see.

WALKERS:
A child, we saw
a child's face,
for an instant, the hint
of his forehead, sharp chin . . .
We trembled, as did the child.
Waves, shards of shapes
flowed in the stones,
bringing alive a relief
that writhes
and sways.

TOWN CHRONICLER:
Or so it seems
to hearts that crave?
That rave?

WALKERS:
Is it simply swelling
in the rock, or could it be
a child's tiny nose?
A mouth opening wide
or grimacing? Or just

a fissure
in the cleft of rock?

A girl? Was it a girl
who loomed above him
and then vanished? Will she return?
A girlish flicker
hovered,
dissipated,
as if the little one had knocked
just for a moment on the doors
of actuality—
then startled.

As she fades, the boy's face changes
right before our eyes. It turns
into the long, fine, gentle
features of a youth.
His profile turns toward us,
slow, with endless wonderment.
He looks straight at us,
two eyebrows
soft arches
in the stone. His eyes
black holes.

TOWN CHRONICLER:
Minute by minute they are losing
their minds. Look, people,
look: It's a wall!
Slabs of rock!
The faces you behold
are merely
phantasms of light,
sleights of shade
and stone—

WALKERS:
But they are so
alive! They flicker
with the flash of smiles,
with questioning and sorrow,
as if those longing, desperate faces
wish to try out
every last expression
one more time,
to thereby taste
the potency
of plundered feelings.

Struck by our own hearts,
our souls wrestled,
struggled to break free,

out of their prison,
to pass from here
to there . . . Seized
by frenzy,
cranes in cages
were our souls,
while in the sky
a flock of birds
passed by,
migrating home.

TOWN CHRONICLER:
It is the longing, I am sure,
it is the longing that deranges
my own mind as well.
Listen to me, listen:
only our longing
sculpts our loved ones, living,
flickering.
Yes, there, look—there!
In the reliefs
of stone—

WALKERS:
And more than anything, the mouths.
Moving, moving constantly, gaping,
rending, twisting,

rounding . . . Perhaps
in supplication?
To whom?
Or imprecation?
Upon whom?

CENTAUR: Damn it all, if only I could be with
them! If only I were there, not sitting here writing
and writing! I would ram the wall and tear it
down, I would break in and I would—

WALKERS:
And their bodies, are they
pushing, driving
at the wall? Fighting? Against whom?
And what? Or struggling
to thrust their way
back here?

TOWN CHRONICLER:
Or like a small child
waking, still addled,
draped in dream, beating
at his mother's chest,
clinging,
beating, beating,
hugging . . .

WALKERS:
We saw an arm,
a slender shoulder, then a knee,
another, then two buds
sprouted, mounded,
a young girl's sharp new breasts.
Above them was her face,
which slowly turned
into a smiling boy's,
the pair of breasts became
two babies' faces,
boy and girl.
Long hands were laid
and ten thin fingers
spread themselves around
the boyish face. His nose,
it seemed, pressed up against
the dimness of a window
as he tried to
penetrate the depths
of darkness
with his gaze.

Was he trying? Did they try
to call us? Or to warn us?
Perhaps we, too,
from there, seemed

merely faint outlines,
fighting our way
out of solid rock—

Terror,
terror fell upon us.
Soon it all will vanish.
We must run now,
sink our faces
in the wall, breach it,
pull them,
tear them
out—

We froze. We did
not move! If only
we could speak to them, we thought,
we'd tell them everything
we did not say when they
still lived. Or else
we'd shout at them
through the lips of the hole
rent in us, through which
our life
seeps out
in throbbing
surges.

CENTAUR: The walking man suddenly fell on his knees at the wall and whispered his son's name. There was no voice in his whisper, only a gaping mouth and torn eyes. In my room, I felt a sharp blade fly over here from there and slice me in two. Through my swoon of pain I heard behind me, from within the piles of objects, the voice of a small child who said quietly, softly murmuring:

BOY:
There is
breath
there
is breath
inside the pain
there is
breath

CENTAUR: I stood up on my feet. I walked around the room. I picked up this or the other object and touched it, stroked it, brought it to my lips. Then I went back and stood at the window. I could see very well using a pair of binoculars I found in one of the piles: the walker's whisper seemed to reap the other walkers. Like him, they, too, fell to their knees, the midwife and the cobbler, the elderly teacher, the net-mender and the duke, the

town chronicler and his wife. And each and every
one of them, each and every one of us, called out,
whispered, to his child:

WALKERS:
Lilli—
Adam? My little
Lilli—Michael—Oh, my child,
my sweet, my lost one—Hanna,
Hanna, look here—Sorry, Michael,
for hitting you—
Adam, it's
Dad—Uwi—
My speck of life—

We awoke
lying on the ground.
The wall
stood no longer.
Perhaps it had never been
there. Perhaps nothing
of what we saw
really was.

But then a strange thought
passed through

all of us,
elusive yet acute,
as if a hand
had stitched us
with a thread: perhaps
when the man
stood up
in his little kitchen
and said:
I have to go there,
perhaps at that same moment
something also shifted
there.
And when
the man began
to walk around himself
in circles
by his house—
they, too,
from there,
began to walk
here,
to the meeting point?

We pictured them
now slightly stooped,

waning,
slowly turning
back.

WALKING MAN:
And he
is dead.
I understand, almost,
the meaning of
the sounds: the boy
is dead.
I recognize
these words
as holding truth.
He is dead,
he is
dead. But
his death,

his death
is not
dead.

CENTAUR:
Yet still it breaks my heart,
my son,
to think

that I have—
that one could—
that I have found
the words.

April 2009–May 2011

Notes

The quote on page III is from e. e. cummings's poem "a clown's smirk in the skull of a baboon." The quote on page 135 is based on Avraham Huss's Hebrew translation of "Orpheus, Eurydice, Hermes," by Rainer Maria Rilke.

ALSO BY
DAVID GROSSMAN

TO THE END OF THE LAND

Just before his release from service in the Israeli army,
Ora's son Ofer is sent back to the front for a major offen-
sive. In a fit of preemptive grief and magical thinking, so
that no bad news can reach her, Ora sets out on an epic
hike in the Galilee. She is joined by an unlikely compan-
ion—Avram, a former friend and lover with a troubled
past—and as they sleep out in the hills, Ora begins to
conjure her son. Ofer's story, as told by Ora, becomes
a surprising balm both for her and for Avram—and a
mother's powerful meditation on war and family.

Fiction/Literature

VINTAGE INTERNATIONAL
Available wherever books are sold.
www.vintagebooks.com